The Detective Airman

by G. H. Teed

Illustrated by Val Reading

First published in the Union Jack,
Series 2, No. 501, 17 May 1913.

Stillwoods Edition

Stillwoods.Blogspot.Ca

Catalogue Details:
Title: The Detective Airman
Author: G. H. Teed (1881-1938)
Illustrated by: Val Reading
First published in the Union Jack, Series 2, No. 501, 17 May 1913.
This Edition by: Stillwoods, 2021
ISBN Canada: 978-1-989788-42-4
Blog: Stillwoods.Blogspot.Ca
Author Blog: http://ghteed.blogspot.com/
Storefront: http://www.lulu.com/spotlight/lulubook22

Keywords: Sexton Blake, British fictional detective, Tinker, Yvonne Cartier

Cautionary Note: This series of books by Stillwoods are intended to make the stories of G. H. Teed, born in New Brunswick Canada, available to collectors and researchers. The editor, or rather digitizer has not altered the original publication.

This story may contain language and racial terms that are not appropriate to today. I apologize for them; I know that the author was using his voice to excite and entertain an adventurous English audience. These works were published from 82 to 110 years ago. Most every work has characters of redeeming ethnicity within.

I hope you enjoy and share these stories; I have.
Doug Frizzle

Sexton Blake—Airman!

A Splendidly Written Tale introducing the Most Topical Subject of To-day, Specially Prepared for Readers of All Ages and of Either Sex.

"Yvonne is the most powerful adventuress of modern times."
(Extract from a letter of a well-known professional Gentleman.)

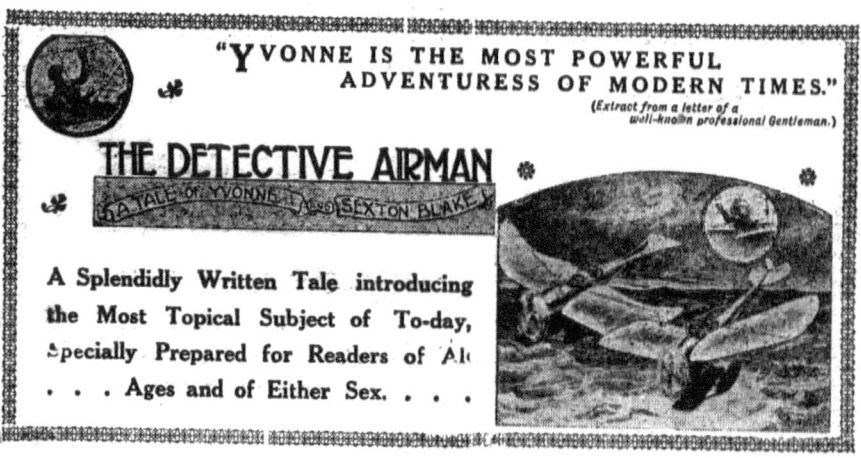

The First Chapter. Mr. Cornelius Patterson Plays a Double Game —Mdlle. Yvonne Takes a Hand.

THE Mastodonic, the latest achievement in the feverish race for the passenger supremacy of the Atlantic, was forging down the English Channel. Her gigantic, powerful engines were whirling unceasingly as she ploughed on through the night, her teeming army of stokers and oilers looking like a horde of modern Ulysses at the feet of a mammoth steel Cyclops.

Up on deck, where only the distant throb of the steel monsters was heard, and the quivering, all-pervading, yet impalpable jar was felt, the passengers lolled in dreamy enjoyment of the heavy summer night.

Some were dancing on the windward side, while the plaintive, distant sounds of a violin indicated the occupation of the saloon by the musical enthusiasts. Bridge and poker devotees lounged in the smoking-room and the divan, alternating their play with frequent sippings from ice clinking glasses.

A few laggards strolled out from the up-to-date restaurant, for the most part pacing slowly up and down the broad promenade, or joining the greatly-preponderating number of white-garbed loungers who lay in shadowy rows, victims of the night's loveliness.

Curving upwards and outwards from the merciless bow, the water rose like twin pillars of sapphire and ivory, opal and pearl, falling into rolling masses of boiling phosphorescence, to conquer with silver wings the giant sinister patches of deadly black.

Further out the silver wings were in their turn conquered and absorbed by the all-pervading black—intense, limitless and terrible in its might. Mirrored in its tossing bowl was the blurred reflection of the night sky which hung like a motionless purple veil studded and splashed with spangles of gold. A faint breeze blended with the steady ship-born wind as the mammoth forged on, stealing with warm embrace into the most shadowy nooks of the deck.

Truly a night for thoughts—a night for dreams and, from the close-drawn chairs in the shadows, a night for the whispers of love.

As the energetic dancers grew tired and strolled around to join in the enjoyment of the languorous night—as the desultory conversation died away, and youthful hands met in the friendly shadow, the slim, white-garbed figure of a girl detached itself from a dark corner of the deck, and strolled slowly to the rail, where she stood leaning over and drinking in the soft air.

A slight stir went through the silent, lounging passengers as her graceful figure was silhouetted against the purple sky, and once again the whispering started, but this time it was confined to the feminine element, and, had a light suddenly been thrown over them, it would have been seen that the whisperers were mostly old or plain.

Like all beautiful women, the girl who leaned over the rail was the target for many feminine shafts born of envy, and their points were not dulled by the fact that her conduct was as reproachless as that of a nun.

As the ship rolled in gentle caress to meet the black, silver-edged lips of the water, the light from the golden spangles in the sky caught her features in a thousand facets, bathing her in seductive lambent hues.

She lifted her face, a triumph of delicate beauty, until all unconsciously her gleaming coils of heavy bronze hair blended with the lighter bronzy of the golden light. She was clad in soft, clinging white, with the daintiest of white shoes on two deliciously-tiny feet. A solitary antique Egyptian scarab decorated her hand, and the green depths of a gigantic emerald rested in perfect harmony against her white throat.

To those whispering envious women—to the admiring, yet baffled men, who, with all their experience and their millions had failed to pierce the armour of her reserve, she was Miss Ford, travelling to New York in the captain's care. But to a tall, stern-faced man in Baker Street, London—Sexton Blake —she was the elusive, charming, and altogether delightful Mademoiselle Yvonne, whose every fibre responded in futile vibration to the touch of his hands, the look in his eyes, the sound of his voice.

She sighed deeply, and rested her chin on her hand. Her thoughts travelled back to the last time she had seen Blake— to his continuous crossing of her path and his domination of every situation. Like puppets on the human stage, she could dominate and move to her bidding every man but one, and that one, not only reversed the situation and dominated her, but, strange to say, she could not bring herself to hate him. On the contrary—

Her thoughts broke off as from the corner of her eye she saw the elaborate carelessness of a strolling man in white, and knew from the blatant innocence of his attitude that he intended to speak to her. Her eyes had been heavy with weariness as she thought of the man who held her heart shackled by his power, but whose own heart-strings failed to respond. They cleared, however, as she watched the approaching man, and an imp of mischief filled them as she watched her victim approach, for victim she intended to make him.

Closer and closer he got, and still she did not turn. Finally, with a painfully-sudden interest in the sky, he approached the rail, and leaned over near her. Apparently utterly unconscious of his presence, Yvonne turned carelessly in the opposite direction, and as a titter of amusement went through the interested spectators of the little drama, Yvonne tripped daintily along the deck, not permitting herself to laugh until she reached a shadowy spot. Her discomfited victim glared viciously at the grinning spectators, and betook himself to the smoking-saloon and poker.

Leaving the alluring deck, and passing through the divan, Yvonne approached the lift with which the newest of the ocean monsters are being equipped.

She smiled in a friendly fashion at the lift boy, and that delighted young man closed the door and sent the lift downwards, to stop with unaccustomed gentleness at her deck. Through several white-walled, heavily-carpeted passages went Yvonne, until she came to a small branch passage.

She opened a door, and entered a richly-furnished suite— sitting-room and sleeping-cabin. They were more contracted in area than her apartments on her own yacht—the Fleur-de-Lys; but even the most blatant of the new millionaires would have found them pleasant for a journey.

Yvonne locked the door, and entered the sleeping-cabin, from which she emerged a few moments later clad in a dark-coloured costume.

Then from a small black bag she drew forth a small square, mahogany box, which looked as though it might be the receptacle of a good-sized traveller's inkstand. At first glance it would have been difficult to distinguish which of its polished sides was the cover; but the puzzle presented no difficulties to Yvonne.

Running her fingers along one edge, she pressed gently half-way down, the result being a tiny click, and the flying open of one side. Inside was revealed a tangle of thin coiled wires, with a gleaming needle of steel in the centre, looking for all the world like a coppery snake with fang out-thrust.

Yvonne gently lifted the needle, pulling slowly until fully a yard of the delicate wire had uncoiled. The bottom, which was visible when the needle and wire had been drawn out, was evidently only half-way down the box, for the space was far more shallow than would have been the case had it extended the full depth. One end of the wire passed through this black partition into what was evidently another compartment, and this fact Yvonne speedily made certain by her next movement.

Leaving the needle and wire to dangle, she turned the box over and once more pressed on an edge.

The opposite side flew open, and at first the contents appeared to be almost similar to those of the other compartment. But as she thrust in her fingers and drew them out again it could be seen that there was a slight difference. Instead of the long, gleaming steel needle, she drew out a tiny miniature receiver in form like those of the ordinary telephone. Like the needle, however, it was attached to a length of copper wire, which in turn was attached to a small battery.

To this also was screwed the end of the other wire, which ran through the division from the needle. Then, with her box in her hand, Yvonne walked over to the large couch which had been placed under the yawning porthole of her sitting-cabin. If her movements before had been curious, they were even more so now. She picked up the needle, and resting one knee on the couch, leaned over against the wall at the head of it. The tiny hole into which she thrust the needle's point would have defied discovery except under the closest scrutiny, but the ease with which she located it proved its position had been made familiar by repeated use.

She thrust the needle through until fully half of it had disappeared into the wall, and then, laying the box and receiver on the couch, she stepped noiselessly across to the switch and turned out the light. Returning to the couch, she placed the box against the wall and lay down, picking up the receiver as she did so. With this against her ear, she lay in motionless silence, her eyes narrowed and her lips slightly parted as she breathed silently.

It had taken Yvonne several weeks of the most careful investigation, and the use of much money, to discover the facts which had started her out on the Mastodonic's maiden trip, and had caused her to pay a big fee in order to secure the particular cabin which she desired.

Naturally, the maiden trip of the newest, biggest, and fastest ocean leviathan had created intense interest, not only in the shipping world, but amongst all classes. This fact, however, was only of passing interest to Yvonne, compared with the fact that it would have as a passenger one Cornelius Patterson.

To the world at large, Cornelius Patterson was simply a shrewd Canadian millionaire—to his own intimate acquaintances, a cold, self-centred man whose heel was heavy, and whose weight had been felt by many since his sudden access to wealth and power after the remarkable rise in Canadian lands.

To Yvonne, however, he was simply one of the men who, years ago in Australia, had denuded herself and her mother of everything in the world, and whose name was the next on her list of revenge. Slowly had she drawn a line through the names preceding it—Vineburg, Pearson, Todd, Kelly, and Morton. It had cost her much money and more skill in order to reach them, but she had succeeded, and although the Todd affair had sent her to Dalemoor Prison from which she had escaped, the fact that Scotland Yard were wanting her did not deter her from going ahead on her plan of revenge.

It was a well-known fact in Europe that Turkey was struggling with a last effort to secure funds for its impoverished treasury with which to continue its ill-fated war with the Balkan allies. It was also a fact, but not so well known, that in her last desperate endeavours, the great gleaming central jewel of the gem-studded throne which had been captured from Persia centuries ago had been removed and taken secretly to Berlin, and on which it was hoped to raise an initial loan.

A huge glass imitation had been set in the throne, and rumour had it, that certain German interests had advanced the Turkish emissary half a million on the famous jewel. Yvonne's agents had discovered, however, that this was incorrect. The jewel called the "Sun's Eye" had, it is true, been taken to Berlin, but an American and Canadian syndicate, represented by Cornelius Patterson, had advanced the loan on it.

Patterson, who was in Europe at the time, had formed his syndicate by cable, and had himself taken charge of the stone on his return to America by the Mastodonic.

Yvonne, after a careful consideration of the details, had decided to get possession of the great jewel if possible, and once her decision was made she acted swiftly. An examination of the passenger-sheet at the shipping-office had disclosed the cabin which Cornelius Patterson had reserved. It seemed a foregone conclusion that he would place the jewel in the care of the purser, but Yvonne, with her usual tenacity of purpose, had resolved to risk no chance to secure it. If no opportunity occurred during the trip, she would have to make the attempt after landing. But even so, she had followed her usual thoroughness. From the moment she had come aboard she had carefully studied the millionaire's movements, and knew by now his every habit.

The tiny hole in the partition between the two cabins through which she had thrust the steel needle came out on the other side underneath the bunk where Patterson slept, and from its position ran no risk of discovery. The thin needle was hollow, and the black partition through which it passed was a sounding-board—the whole outfit of box, wires, battery, and receiver, being a most compact and complete instrument which collected every sound in Patterson's cabin, and transmitted them through the needle and along the wire, to be magnified to clarity and distinctness, and thence to the receiver against Yvonne's ear.

And it was because she knew the millionaire would retire early that Yvonne had deserted the charms of the deck, and began the usual listening to her neighbour's movements and mutterings.

For fully half an hour no sound travelled along the thin wires of her delicate instrument, but her patience was at length rewarded. She heard her neighbour's cabin door open, and then along the faithful recorder came the sound of a turning key. The movements after that were muffled and shuffling like the noise of a trunk being dragged out from under a bunk, but as she heard her neighbour muttering brokenly, Yvonne held her breath and strained to listen.

"There's no better time than right now," came the voice of the millionaire, muttering to himself as he worked with the straps of the trunk. "The captain and purser have both seen it, and can swear I had it with me; then, when the purser comes to get it to-morrow and take charge of it for me, I'll discover it's gone. No one dreams that this trunk contains a little form of transportation which will escape the sharpest eye. Ah, you beauty —steady, steady! You can go free in a minute, but there is a little package to be attached to your leg first."

Each word of her neighbour's monologue had been heard by

Yvonne in puzzled surprise. She could gather no meaning from the strange remarks. That he was speaking of the great jewel she felt certain, but what did he mean by "transportation which would escape the sharpest eye"?

At that moment a peculiar sound came to her ears, and as she heard it she laid the instrument down and leaped softly to her feet, breathing quickly.

"Good heavens!" she breathed; everything made clear in a flash. "Is it possible?"

She hastily picked up the instrument again and listened, her lips parting in a smile as she heard the words which the tiny needle collected and sent along.

"There, my beauty, stop your flapping!" Patterson was saying. "You'll be free in a minute, and can fly back home. But you must carry cargo with you and it must be secured, for after all my elaborate plans, I don't want to risk having it drop into the Channel."

Yvonne again dropped the receiver, and began working feverishly. First she sped to the corner of her cabin and unstrapped a bundle of parasols and umbrellas. Selecting a black umbrella with a long handle, she then drew a golf-club from a bag which also stood in the corner. Stepping swiftly across to the couch again, she laid them down, and from her black bag drew a small coil of wire. She then placed the handle of the golf-club against the handle of the umbrella, and with the hand of an expert bound them firmly together with the wire.

When she had finished she had a remarkable-looking umbrella, for by the addition of the golf-club she had lengthened its handle some three feet. Still moving noiselessly, she thrust it partly through the open porthole, and followed it with her head and shoulders. Patterson's port was lit up, but the shadow which crossed it from time to time indicated that its occupant was moving about. A moment later it grew still more obscured, and a hand appeared holding something which was struggling and fluttering.

As her eyes perceived it, and she saw her suspicions were correct, Yvonne released the catch on the umbrella, and firmly clutching the business end of the golf-club, thrust it outwards and upwards as far as she could. The wind caught it and opened it completely, just as the hand in the next porthole released its struggling prisoner.

For a moment the fluttering object poised, and then rose to

freedom; but, carried along by the ship, the umbrella came directly over, and, as it rose, Yvonne drew in sharply until her free hand reached the release of the umbrella. Too late the bird saw the dark object descending. Its impetus carried it upwards within the clutch of the black descending cloud, and as its wings fluttered against the ribs of the umbrella, the top closed. Once more a prisoner, the bird struggled to get free; but the trap was strong, and a moment later Yvonne had drawn the umbrella back through the porthole, and stepped from the couch to the floor.

Laying down her hastily-devised trap, with its prisoner inside, she turned back to close the port, listening for a moment as a scraping noise sounded from the next porthole, followed by a splash.

"That's the cage which he had concealed in his trunk, I suppose," she murmured softly, brushing the flying spray from her forehead. She closed the port, and turned again to the umbrella, whose soft folds were heaving and bulging as her prisoner struggled.

"And now, Mr. Cornelius Patterson,"—she smiled softly— "we'll just see what cargo your aerial messenger was carrying."

She cautiously opened the umbrella, and thrust in her hand, drawing it out a moment later with a firm hold on her captive.

"So, so," she nodded, as she looked on the soft feathers and graceful lines of a powerfully-built homing-pigeon. "Very clever, Mr. Patterson, and it is a pity your aerial post was interrupted. Steady, you darling; I wouldn't hurt you for worlds. But I must see what that little package is which my neighbour has tied to your leg."

For a moment she held the soft, feathery bundle against her cheek, petting it and soothing it until it grew quiet under her touch. Then, holding it firmly with one hand, she began unfastening the tiny package from its leg. After five minutes' work it dropped into her lap, and she began rapidly unwrapping the paper which covered it. As the last covering fell off she drew in a quick breath. There, scintillating in a thousand flashes of gleaming fire, lay the great "Sun's Eye," which had provided the Turks with funds to continue the war, and which, as she had discovered only this night, was temptation enough to cause Cornelius Patterson to lay elaborate plans in order to possess it himself and bluff the world it had been stolen.

For Yvonne had read in a flash his purpose. The fact that he was secretly sending the jewel to England by a homing-pigeon told her enough to make her suspicious; but the words she had heard had added light to the matter, and again she smiled as she thought of her successful frustration of his plans.

She laid the jewel down on her lap, and was preparing to release the bird when her eyes caught sight of some written words on the last paper wrapping which she had taken off. Sinking back, she picked it up and read:

"On receipt, leave at once and meet me as arranged. Advise arrival by wireless code. Be careful."

That was all. It contained neither address nor signature, but Yvonne laughed softly as she studied the metal band around the pigeon's leg.

"No. 1373 S," she murmured. "I suppose that is your registered number. I'll just jot it down, at any rate, and as soon as I have written another message you can start on your long journey."

She tucked the pigeon under her arm, and going to the black bag pulled out a small pad and pencil. She wrote only a few words, and, after folding up the note, carefully attached it to the pigeon's leg.

Then, after once more petting and caressing it, she opened the port and released it. For a moment it poised on outspread wings, and then, driven sideways by the wind, rose in ever-widening circles until it became a mere speck against the night sky, and disappeared a moment later as the great leviathan pounded on its way.

Then Yvonne went through a very strange procedure. Picking up the instrument which had served her so well, she dropped it through the open porthole into the sea. After that she drew out her trunk from under the couch and opened it. A hasty examination revealed several instruments —appliances of steel and silver which she ruthlessly sent after the instrument.

A scrutiny of the umbrella-handle showed that the wire had cut into its dull surface, and, careful as always, the umbrella and golf-stick followed the other things. From the trunk she next drew a long, narrow cork affair which might have been a giant yard of French bread except for the material of which it was made. Laying this on the couch, Yvonne again reached into the trunk, and drew forth three small steel globes the size of a cricket ball. From the surface of each projected a tiny key, and on the opposite side from the key a small square knob. Next, she lifted out three small wooden floats in each of which was a small square hole into which fitted the knobs of the globes.

Yvonne next proceeded to turn the key of each one, after the manner of winding a clock, and then, laying them on the couch beside the long cork float, she locked the trunk and thrust it back.

After a final look around, Yvonne crossed and entered the sleeping-cabin, and when she returned her costume had been replaced by a short tweed golf-skirt and light canvas shoes. Her heavy bronze hair was enclosed in a tight-fitting bathing-cap, and a bathing-jersey took the place of a blouse.

Thus equipped, she drew a roll of notes from the black bag, and picking up the three floats, to which she had attached the steel globes, hooked them to her jersey by tiny hooks which had been placed in the end of each.

Then crossing to the switch she plunged the cabin in darkness and returned to the couch. Climbing up, she put her head through the porthole and listened intently for some moments.

The star-studded sky was now obscured by scudding clouds, and the silver-and-black of the sea had turned to a leaden grey. No sound floated down from the decks above, and as eight bells struck on the fo'c's'le she knew the passengers had sought their berths. Only the officer on the bridge and the watch would be about, and Yvonne gave a sigh of relief as the scudding clouds grew thicker

She drew back and picked up the cork float, which she thrust through the porthole. Pulling herself up, she squirmed through after it, and twisted around in order to hang by one hand from the rim of the open port. It was fortunate for her purpose that her cabin was near the water, for had it been high up, unless the ship was rolling considerably, a splash would have been inevitable. But the sea was still, gently moving in long, rolling lines, and as the great ship slowly sank downwards Yvonne waited until it paused a moment before returning, and then, clutching her float, dropped silently into the black water beneath.

She lost no time in pushing her float in front of her and striking out with all her strength as soon as she came to the surface, for she had no desire to be drawn near those mammoth whirling propellers by the leviathan's suction. At the same time she had to swim noiselessly in order to avoid the eagle eyes of the watch on deck; but the smoothness of the sea assisted her, and as the stem of the great, lighted, floating castle swept past she rested on her cork float and gazed after it.

"Perhaps I'll wish I was back," she murmured. "But if uncle has followed instructions there will be no risk. If not, I'm afraid no ingenuity will get me out of this; but there's time enough for that. I'll start the signals going."

Still resting on the float which was buoyantly riding the long, rolling swell, Yvonne detached the three globes from her jersey and set them on the surface beside the float. By this time the Mastodonic was a blurred tangle of lights, and before releasing the three globes Yvonne waited until the vessel grew even more indistinct. Then she gave the key on each steel globe a rapid turn backwards, a buzzing sound followed, and as she pulled the keys out and threw them away a tiny wire appeared in the aperture left.

With a strong heave she sent them out one after the other to ride the waves at a safe distance, and then covered her eyes with her hands. It was well she did so, for barely had the floats settled in their new resting-place than the tiny wires blazed out a blinding flash of vivid blue. They died down as the delicate machines inside each globe cut off the power.

Again they blazed out with a blinding flash, to die down once more for their momentary extinction before flashing for the third time. Then they went out for a longer spell, and as they lit up with a less blinding flare to burn steadily, Yvonne removed her hand from her eyes and began anxiously gazing upwards into the cloud-hung night.

For fully five minutes she gazed before her features relaxed, and then far distant in the black sky, in the direction of the now invisible Mastodonic, there appeared three blue lights, which went out almost immediately. But Yvonne knew her signal had been seen, and that the three steadily burning wires would guide her uncle to her.

Barely three minutes later a long, narrow, graceful shape appeared above her, flying at a low elevation, and as it settled down noiselessly the shape of a slim waterplane could be made out. A soft hail floated down to Yvonne, and a moment later, like a giant bird, the waterplane settled on the waves close behind the floating girl.

It was a radical advance on the more cumbersome form of machine. Built of a light alloy of metal, with wings outspread, it could rise by a central lifting propeller without any preliminary run. Built on gigantic lines, as compared with other machines, it was capable of tremendous lifting-power, in addition to a heavy cargo allowance. Every exposed inch was finished in silver-blue, which in daylight blended with the sky, making the machine totally invisible from the ground when only a few hundred yards up.

The engine was of a hundred horse-power, and one of the most reliable she had been able to purchase.

With a light but very effective type of float attached to the chassis, it could be used as a waterplane, and, with floats lifted, rise gracefully from the water, to disappear rapidly in the upper strata.

When leaving on the Mastodonic, Yvonne had instructed Graves, her uncle, and Captain Vaughan, to follow with the yacht, and watch for her signal in case she were unsuccessful in her purpose during the trip.

Even in mid-ocean she would have risked putting her daring plan into operation; but luck was with her, and well was it that the men on the yacht had watched closely for her signal from the very start.

As the long shape floated gracefully beside her, she pushed the float around to the side.

"Are you all right, Yvonne?" asked Graves anxiously, reaching down his hand to her and helping her aboard.

"Yes, thanks!" laughed Yvonne. "Wet to the skin, but successful."

"Do you mean to say that you got it?" exclaimed Graves and the captain together.

"You don't imagine I would take this midnight swim unless I had, do you?" replied Yvonne. "It was lucky you followed my instructions to the letter. If you hadn't, I would have been in a nice position riding around on that float all night, with inquisitive fishes nibbling at my toes."

Graves laughed.

"You are bewildering, Yvonne. But here, put this heavy coat around you, or you will catch cold. I've got a Thermos flask full of hot lemon for you. Drink it! It will keep off a chill."

Yvonne got into the heavy coat and drank the hot liquid, while Captain Vaughan steered the waterplane around, in order that Graves could pick up the cork float and globes, which were still burning with the steady blue light.

Then the captain turned.

"Shall I drive her back to land, mademoiselle?" he asked.

Yvonne nodded.

"Yes. Not too high, though. It will be cold. Take this seat, uncle, and let me sit there. The wind won't catch me so much."

"Tell me, Yvonne," said Graves as he changed, "how did you succeed. I'm keen to know."

Yvonne lit a cigarette before replying, and then watched the black waves as the great wings spread out and they rose silently in the air.

"Well," began Yvonne, turning back to Graves, "in the first place, our friend, Mr. Cornelius Patterson, hasn't improved since the old days in Australia. I don't know the details of his plan, but this I do know. He intended getting rid of the Sun's Eye himself, and then giving the alarm that he had been robbed."

"Did he have an accomplice aboard?"

Yvonne laughed gaily.

"I hardly think one could call 'it' an accomplice."

Then she related to the chuckling Graves how the millionaire had taken a homing-pigeon, concealed in his trunk, and had tied the great jewel to it, and sent it back to England to some unknown accomplice there. How she had caught the bird, and secured the jewel and note, and had sent it on its interrupted journey with another note tied to its leg.

Graves laughed in delighted appreciation, while the captain smiled appreciatively as he guided the machine through the night.

"By Jove, Yvonne," drawled Graves, "that was about as rich as I've ever heard! But, I say, what did you write in the note you sent?"

Yvonne laughed gaily.

"I simply wrote, 'What price the Sun's Eye?' and I would give something to read the wireless our friend Mr. Cornelius Patterson will get when the note reaches its destination."

Tossing her cigarette away, Yvonne drew the folds of the heavy coat about her and leaned back. Her eyes closed, and in five minutes she was asleep, her hair was falling in distracting waves about her forehead as the wind caught it, and her lips parted with a soft girlish smile as she floated away into pleasant dreams.

Little did she look like a world-famous adventuress, and Graves, cynic though he was, sighed heavily as he watched the unconscious appeal of her girlishness. He turned to see the hardened captain looking at her with the affectionate look of a father.

"She's just like a tired child!" said the captain gruffly as he turned back to the steering-wheel.

Graves nodded, but said nothing, and silence reigned as the long, slim shape tore on through the night, the black sky above and the water beneath.

The Second Chapter.   The Great Circuit Race—A Message from the Night Sky.

NEVER did Hendon Flying Grounds present a more gala appearance than on the day which would see the end of the great circuit race for fame and a fortune. Several days previously the great meeting had been inaugurated with the start of the race.

Starting from Hendon, the 'planes were to fly to Land's End, and from there circuit east over the Channel, thence up to John o' Groats. From there they were to make Belfast, return over the Channel, circle Eddystone, and return to Hendon. In itself the race presented difficulties of the most trying description.

A great portion of the course lay over water, and, to add to the difficulties, each pilot must carry a passenger, and a hundred pounds weight in addition. With air conditions ideal it was a gruelling test, but with the rapid strides of other nations in aerial navigation, England was forced into keen competition, and the great circuit test had been devised in order to choose a standard machine on which to concentrate.

Five all-British machines had started on the race, and ever since they had risen and disappeared with a whirr and a roar, Hendon had been packed each day to watch the minor flights and tests of lesser machines. Little word had been heard from any of the five starters since they had left, and little hope was felt that all of them would finish. All had been reported at Land's End; then one at a time they had been heard of as they flew up the eastern coast.

Then came a long silence, until word came through from Belfast that two had landed in the teeth of a gale. No word had been heard of the other three, and opinions were freely expressed that the gale had probably sent them into the sea.

Alter replenishing their fuel and lubricating tanks, the two machines had braved the gale, and started once more on the last lap around Eddystone. Not a word of any kind had been heard since, but if schedule time was kept to, this day would see the finish, providing there were still any left in the race. No one had eyes for the evolutions being performed overhead. Every head was turned southwards to catch the first glimpse of the expected machines.

Now and then an aviator flew southwards to scout about for the expected racers, but each time he returned with no news, and the excitement of the crowd grew intense as the afternoon waned.

Four o'clock came, and still no sign. Five would see the end of the time limit, and if they arrived after that hour, all their long, dangerous flight would go for nothing.

Half-past four drew round, but barely had the fatal half begun, when, far away in the south, a tiny speck, no bigger than a swallow, appeared.

Was it only another bird like these which many times that afternoon had raised false hopes? If so, it was certainly of a larger species, and as it grew nearer, heading straight up for Hendon, a terrific cheer went up. It must be the first of the returning circuit racers. All the scouts had come to earth, and no other machines were known to be out.

On and on it came, ever growing larger until the first faint throb of its engines was heard. Then the more experienced eyes recognised the outlines of the machine, and powerful glasses read the big, white number painted on the underpart of the wings. There was no need for the excited crowd to ask who drove it. As the first user of the glasses shouted:

"It's No. 4!" the cry was taken up, and repeated from end to end.

"Who's driving No. 4?"

"Sexton Blake, on his own machine!"

A deafening cheer arose.

Blake's name was shouted wildly, programmes were waved madly, and the slim, grey shape of Sexton Blake's machine grew ever nearer. As the throb of the engine stopped, and it volplaned gracefully to earth, the enthusiasm broke all bounds. Shouting and cheering, the crowd surged forward, endangering themselves and the aviator as he came to earth.

Almost in their centre he landed, and only the ceaseless work of the officials kept them from swarming completely over machine, aviator, and passenger in their excitement.

Blake, black with grease and oil, was helped from the machine by willing hands. He staggered with weariness, and answered their questions hoarsely.

"I don't know where the others are. Haven't seen a machine since I left Belfast in the teeth of a seventy-mile gale. But see to my passenger. I think he's asleep."

It was true!

Tinker, who had gone as Blake's passenger, lay crouched in his seat, sound asleep, worn out with the strain of the long journey and racking fight with the elements. They lifted him out, and followed the staggering Blake into the hangar, while the crowd cheered itself hoarse over the man who, by his great flight, had won a fortune. Fame was his already.

Regardless of the crowd or his greasy state, Blake signed to his mechanic to look after the machine, and, stumbling to a pile of canvas in the corner of the hangar, he dropped down, his eyes closing in the deep sleep of utter weariness almost before his head had touched the rough couch. They laid the sleeping Tinker beside him, and while every paper in the country came out with a special edition over the great race, the man who had won it and his passenger lay unconscious of everything.

.   .   .   .   .

Early the next morning Blake and Tinker were awake, and on their way to Baker Street in the big grey car. After a bath and change, they felt better, and Blake, setting Tinker to work opening letters, ran through his mail rapidly. Noon saw them again on their way to Hendon, for a vigorous speed test was to come off, and Blake was determined to give his machine a full test of every description.

"I say, guv'nor," remarked Tinker, as they wound their way through the crowded vehicles which circled the ground, "it's going to be a bully day for the flight. The Grey Panther will be getting all it wants."

"It can stand it, my lad," laughed Blake. "As far as a test of strength goes, the circuit we finished yesterday proves the worth of the system of wing attachment which I am trying out; but the flight to-day will require speed and sharp work to locate the battleship. The last race which comes off in two days' time will be purely a speed race from Hendon to Eiffel Tower, in Paris, and return. We'll go in for that, too, if the Grey Panther hangs together."

"We are having a week from work, guv'nor, but this flying is as much strain as following up a case."

It should be explained that the race on which the intrepid Blake was entering this day after his magnificent win of the great circuit, was a flight from Hendon to a super-Dreadnought which was stationed off Land's End.

A large platform had been arranged over the after part of the battleship, and the test was to carry despatches from Hendon, the arrival of the aeroplane to be notified by wireless. There was no specified time for returning, but after a rest, the aviator could choose his own time, providing his leaving on the return journey was notified by wireless.

Only a general idea of the whereabouts of the battleship was given, and, in addition to great speed being required, the aviator would have to scout about in the air and pick up the ship. The test appealed to Blake, and after his success in the grand circuit, he decided to enter it, and if the machine hung out, go in for the final event, a speed race to Paris and back.

Consequently he was on the ground early, and, stopping his car beside the hangar which sheltered his monoplane— the Grey Panther—he and Tinker got into overalls, and with the mechanic, began going over every inch of the machine.

"What time will you start, sir?" asked the mechanic, as Blake twanged a wing stay with the finger of an expert.

"Oh, I don't know, Barrow!" replied Blake. "I saw Gordon landing in his Bleriot as I drove in, and he tells me the air is full of pockets, and choppy. If we finish with the machine by sunset, I may start then. In any event, I'll make a preliminary flight and test the air currents.

"By the way, how many others entered?"

"Only one besides yourself, sir. They thought it would be a lone hand until they heard you had decided to try it."

Blake laughed.

"Who is the other man, Barrow?"

"Whitcomb, sir. He's driving a biplane, and says he'll try and start at three. He's taking his mechanic as passenger, sir."

"Ah, if that's the case, I won't leave before evening, in any event. Any news heard of the other machines in the circuit race, Barrow?"

"Gardener returned to Belfast sir, and Cartwright came to earth on the west coast of Scotland. They haven't heard anything from the other two, sir."

"I'm sorry to hear that," said Blake gravely. "I'm afraid the gale in the North Sea has caught them. Tinker and I had our work cut out to get through. Just give me a hand here, Barrow, and we'll tighten up this joint."

Two hours later word came that Whitcomb, in his Farman, had

made a preliminary flight, and was starting on his long run for the battleship at four. Blake and Tinker dropped their tools and went outside where the aviator was running over the machine preliminary to starting.

"Well, Blake." he smiled through his goggles, as Blake approached, "I thought I was the only one until I heard you were going.. Are you after all the glory?"

"Oh, no!" laughed Blake, shaking hands. "But, you see, you are driving a machine which has been tested for speed, strength, and endurance, while mine has only had the test of the circuit race. I want to put her through the whole thing, and then I can tell just what I've got."

"They say she's a wonder, Blake," remarked Whitcomb enviously. "I'm blest if I see how you find time to fool with flying when you seem to be working on cases night and day!"

"Oh, Tinker and I get through quite a few experiments in the lab., and beyond a preliminary flight, I hadn't the faintest notion what my machine could do. You're leaving at four, are you?"

"Yes, and you?"

"I intended leaving about sunset, but I haven't quite decided; I may wait until midnight."

At that moment Blake's mechanic beckoned to him, and, shaking hands with his solitary competitor, and wishing him luck, Blake hurried away, followed by Tinker after he had compared a few notes on air currents with Whitcomb.

Tinker had developed into a most enthusiastic airman. Under Blake's tutelage, he was rapidly picking up a thorough knowledge of aerial navigation, and the lad had watched the growth of the Grey Panther from the plans born of Blake's brain to its present graceful, speedy lines.

He knew every bolt and nut and stay, and on necessity could have under-studied Blake in driving it. He lost no opportunity of comparing notes with other aviators, and the lad's frank, sunny ways had won him a host of friends on the flying ground. After shaking hands with Whitcomb, he hurried into the hangar, where he found Blake fuming over a snapped stay.

The mechanic had thought to improve on Blake's tinkering, with the result that he had overstrained. It meant a long two hours to replace it, and then a fairly long flight to test it before risking the journey out over the Atlantic.

Round after round of cheers told them Whitcomb was starting, and Tinker lifted the flap of the hangar to see the biplane wheeling in ever-widening circles like a great bird, until finally, Whitcomb, reaching the thousand-foot level, threw out a flag, on which was written "Good-bye," and, heading his machine west, was soon a tiny speck in the blue.

It was after seven before Blake was satisfied with the condition of the Grey Panther, but late as it was in the day, the crowd was as numerous as it had been when Whitcomb got away.

Word had gone round that Sexton Blake, winner of the grand circuit race, was also in for the test, and that had been sufficient to keep them.

Cheers and questions greeted Blake, as he and Tinker wheeled the 'plane out. Blake good-naturedly held up his hand, and, picking up a megaphone from one of the officials, turned to the crowd.

"Thank you, my friends!" he shouted. "I was too fagged yesterday, to say anything. I heard several asking what time I intended getting away. We are going to make a preliminary flight now, and if everything seems satisfactory, we will start in about two hours, after we have had something to eat?"

Renewed cheers broke out as Blake finished and returned the megaphone. Then, assisted up by the mechanic, he took his seat before the driving-wheel, and took the waterproof covering off the chart and compass. Tinker followed him in, and as the mechanic started the powerful engine, the long, slim Grey Panther ran ahead easily for a short distance.

Then, as Blake slightly canted the wings, the 'plane rose gracefully, in gradually-widening spirals, until they were up a thousand feet. Blake banked slightly, and started sweeping around in a great circle, until he was heading east. Then headed straight, and, like a great winged arrow, shot away into the growing dusk. The brilliant arc-lamps were blazing when they returned and volplaned back to earth, satisfied with the flight.

It was now full night, and overhead the stars blazed brilliantly.

A hurried meal was consumed while they sat in the machine, and after replenishing the fuel and oil-tanks, the engine was once more started. The crowd had hung on to watch the start, and not until the grey shape with her two muffled occupants was lost in the starry realms above did the cheers die away.

"What's the general direction, guv'nor?" asked Tinker, turning up his collar and gazing at the swiftly-passing lights far below.

"We will drive dead south for a bit, and then change to a westerly direction. That ought to put us in the neighbourhood of the warship by daylight."

Almost as Blake spoke they rushed towards a revolving light beneath the last outpost of the land. Far away a few glowing spots indicated the presence of other lights, but though flying at a moderate pace, the land dropped away behind with almost uncanny suddenness, and they were left with that indefinable feeling of being the only beings in a vast limitless expanse of great hanging stars above, and tossing, black water beneath, broken only by the steady drone of the Gnome, and the business-like whir of the propeller.

On clearing the land, they hit a down-Channel breeze, and Blake canted the planes, sending the machine up to the two-thousand-foot level. They found, however, that the lower current, though strong, was steady and more reliable than the "pockety" higher level.

Suddenly below them appeared a brilliantly-lighted steamer ploughing on her way, and in a spirit of reckless test in manoeuvring, Blake sent the Grey Panther volplaning down, and circled within a few yards of her excited passengers.

Then, turning, he continued on, and finding the lower level steady flying, stuck to it as he again shot westwards. For two hours they hummed on through the night without speaking, and Blake smiled as he saw Tinker dozing. The pilot's seat and the passenger's seat of the Grey Panther were built to face each other—the glass-framed chart being in front of Tinker, but on account of its pivoted hinges easily accessible to Blake.

The steering-wheel and levers occupied a very small space immediately in front of him; the result being a much more workable arrangement than the ordinary method of having the passenger facing the same way. He was just starting to rise again to the thousand foot, when through the night came a small, whitish object, which struck him with some force in the chest, and dropped fluttering at their feet. Blake grunted from the impact, and started to call Tinkers attention to the fact by tramping on the lad's toe. The fluttering object at his feet, however, awoke the lad, and he stared down in amazement.

"Crumbs, guv'nor! What is it —a seagull? How did it get in

here?"

"We ran into it!" shouted Blake. "Pick it up, and if it isn't injured, throw it over again!"

Tinker bent and picked up the bird, which was flapping about in a crippled manner. As he did so his eyes opened wide with amazement, and, holding it firmly, he held it up for Blake to see.

"Look, guv'nor!" he called. "It's a pigeon, and a homer, too!"

Blake leaned forward quickly.

"See if it is carrying any message, Tinker!" he said. "It's strange for it to be about here, but someone may be sending it from a passenger steamer with a farewell message. Did Whitcomb carry any with him?"

Tinker shook his head, and held the bird while he began searching for any message. As Blake expected, he found one tied securely to the bird's leg, and steadied the struggling pigeon between his knees while he undid it.

Blake divided his attention between the machine and watching Tinker, but, as he saw the lad open the note to read it with puzzled brow by the light of the chart-lamp, he released one hand and held it out for the paper.

"I can't make anything of it!" shouted Tinker. "Seems to refer to a horse-race."

Blake signed to him to swing the chart-lamp around to him, and by the light he read:

"What price Sun's Eye?"

For a long moment he gazed at the words, and then, releasing the map-holder, dropped the note inside.

"Has the pigeon got a band on its leg?" he asked.

Tinker nodded and swung the chart-lamp back.

"Yes, 1873 S."

"Is it hurt?" went on Blake.

"Its wing seems to be injured," replied the lad.

Blake nodded.

"Put it in the grub-locker, Tinker, until morning. We'll go into matters then. Turn on the searchlight. I think we'll get it pretty dark, and from those scudding clouds it looks like a stiff blow coming on. Get out some sandwiches and a bottle of tea. We will eat while we can!"

It was well they did, for Blake's prognostications were correct, and barely had Tinker put the bottle back with their imprisoned bird, and turned on the powerful searchlight, than the blow came and Blake shot up to a higher level.

For a bare moment he seemed to see far, far away on the black, watery stretch, three blue lights blaze up three times, and then go down to burn less brightly. He had half an idea of changing his course and investigating, but at that moment the Grey Panther veered dangerously in the air-pocket, and it needed all his attention to keep her head into the wind.

By the time he had discovered the wind was only on the higher levels, and that by flying low, he escaped it, the blue lights had disappeared.

A vague, shadowy shape seemed to shoot past them a moment later, but if it was a 'plane, the noise of its engines were drowned by their own. So quickly did it disappear, that Blake thought he must be mistaken. Half an hour later, as dawn was breaking, they passed the brilliantly lighted "Mastodonic," and Blake, making a rapid mental calculation which he verified by his distance-register, knew he must be near the battleship.

He changed his course, and, as the sun came up like a great golden orange out of the waves, he began sweeping in ever-widening circles in a comprehensive all-seeing course which must eventually pick up the battleship.

The Third Chapter. *Breakfast on the Thor —Another Message from the Air—Blake Makes a Move.*

"THERE she is! There she is, guv'nor!"

Tinker was leaning over the side with a pair of glasses glued to his eyes, and one hand pointing southwards, while he shouted excitedly.

Blake turned his head, and with his sleeve rubbed the mist from his goggles. It was some time after sun-up, and since the great disc had changed the black waters to leaping silver-edged platinum, Blake had been flying in great circles in an endeavour to pick up the battleship which would mean the end of their flight.

Tinker was right, it was the super-Dreadnought Thor, and as Blake's eyes made out the landing platform over the stem, he swung the Grey Panther around, banking slightly, and then, straight as an arrow, shot southwards. As they drew nearer they could make out Whitcomb's Farman, which had already landed, and from the efforts being made to push it aside, and give Blake a clear landing, he knew they had been sighted. Judging his distance to a fraction, Blake shut off the engine, and volplaned down in a great curve, ever drawing nearer and hearer the platform, which looked more like a tiny plaster on a grey rock than a landing platform.

Suddenly it seemed to jump to meet them, and Blake, again banking, swung once more before putting the Grey Panther's nose to it.

But he hadn't won the grand circuit race without knowing his machine's every move, and, as it swung about on the last volplane, they dropped gently, and, with a jar which would barely have broken an egg, they landed and ran forward into the stopping net. It was a pretty piece of work which on land would have brought its reward of admiration, but on the landing platform of a battleship in mid-ocean, it was a masterpiece of judgment and handling, and Whitcomb showed his good sportsmanship by leading the cheering which rolled from aft, forward, and back again.

Blake and Tinker tumbled out, and beginning with Commander Villiers, had to shake hands all round.

"Blake—Blake," laughed the commander, shaking an admonitory finger at the greasy, goggled detective, "what next will you be taking on? But when Britain needs a cool hand for despatches, I'll see that you are raked out of your den in Baker Street and put into service."

"That's exactly why I am spending so much time on the matter," smiled Blake. "It is my country first and always," he added, more soberly.

"I say, Blake," remarked Whitcomb, who had been trying to make himself heard for several minutes, "what was your time?"

"Exactly what time was at when I struck the ship?" asked Blake.

"Five forty-three to the second!" replied Lieutenant Bruce, whose duty it had been to act as timekeeper.

"Well, we left Hendon about midnight. But hasn't the wireless come through yet? It would give the exact moment."

"Yes, I have it," remarked Lieutenant Bruce. "I didn't announce the time of your leaving until you should arrive. You left Hendon at twelve-twenty exactly, and that makes your trip consume just five hours and twenty-three minutes."

"What was your time, Whitcomb?" asked Blake.

"You have beaten me outwards by six minutes," laughed Whitcomb good naturedly. "But I'll beat you going back. I've got the hang of this biplane now, and I'll drive like sixty devils!"

"You'll have to do better than that," replied Blake. "I intend driving like seventy or even eighty!"

Laughing and joking they turned, Blake under the guidance of a steward to get a hot bath before breakfasting with the commander and officers in the mess-room, and Tinker into the charge of several admiring middies, who insisted on every detail of the trip being gone over and over, and when they discovered he had also made the trip with Blake around the grand circuit—well, the flood of excited questions can be imagined.

Blake, thorough as always, had not forgotten their feathered captive, and the strange manner in which they had collided with it during the night.

Stopping, he spoke to one of the engine-room assistants, who was looking after the machines, and warned him about the injured pigeon in the grub locker. The man promised to look after it, and after breakfast Blake intended examining it in order to see if its injured wing could be mended, or if it would be more merciful to put it out of its pain.

The strange, almost frivolous words of the note, had caused him much thought during the long, silent night journey; but although the reference to the Sun's Eye brought to his mind the jewel which had been the recent talk of Europe, he could not see where there was any connection, and was almost inclined to agree with Tinker that it must refer to a horse-race.

But running into a homing pigeon far out at sea was too remarkable an occurrence to be dismissed without investigation, and after he had satisfied the conditions of the race, Blake intended to look more closely into the strange message which had come to them through the night.

Little did he know how that modern wonder, the wireless system, was to start him on the investigation far sooner than he dreamed.

After a hot bath and a change, a steward conducted him past the middies' mess, where Tinker was guest of honour, into the officers' mess, where Blake was shown to a seat on the commander's right.

Whitcomb sat on his left, and down each side of the table ranged the bronzed, energetic officers of the Thor. Their very faces, clean-cut and vivid with the stamp of the sailor, spoke well for England, and Blake knew every man of them would dash into the teeth of death with the same intrepid nonchalance with which they broke their eggs.

It was a merry breakfast; Blake was famous as a conversationalist, and while seeming to dominate the situation, he was, in reality, keeping the ball rolling up and down the table. Like Tinker with the middies, he had to recount the details of that gruelling race around the grand circuit, and when he finished, Whitcomb related an experience which he had had over the English Channel, when, by colliding with another machine, both men and 'planes had gone tumbling into the water far below.

Breakfast was over—at least, in the officers' mess—and pipes and cigars were going around the table, when the wireless operator entered, and saluting, passed a long message to Commander Villiers.

"What's this?" asked the commander.

"It's a news item through to the Press from the Mastodonic. I picked it up, and thought you might wish to see it. It's rather remarkable."

"Very well," replied the commander. "Pardon, gentlemen, I'll just see what it says."

The conversation began again, but as the commander uttered an ejaculation they broke off, and looked inquiringly at him.

"Just listen to this!" he exclaimed. "If it's true—and it must be—

it is certainly a remarkable occurrence.

" 'Ss. Mastodonic.

" 'Mid-ocean.

"'A remarkable occurrence has taken place on board the Mastodonic during night. Mr. Cornelius Patterson, the Canadian millionaire, who is a passenger, is, by his own statement, head of the syndicate which advanced the Turkish emissaries in Berlin half a million pounds on the jewel known as the "Sun's Eye." Last evening he made arrangements with the purser to have it taken care of on the journey, but put off getting it until this morning.

" 'When he opened his trunk and looked in the cashbox in which he carried it, the jewel had disappeared, and it is feared that it was stolen during the night. Mr. Patterson is positive that he placed it in the cashbox on retiring, and had it out only a few hours previously to show to the captain. A thorough search has failed to reveal it, and Captain Brown has put the ship's detectives on the matter.

"' On top of this, a lady passenger has been discovered missing. Miss Ford, who was travelling to New York, and, who evoked the admiration of the whole ship by her remarkable beauty, cannot be found. On knocking at her cabin this morning, the stewardess got no reply, and on entering she discovered everything in order. But the bunk had not been slept in, and the lady was missing. Miss Ford was very reserved, and had no intimate acquaintance on board, although nominally under the captain's care. Owing to this, it is not known whether she had any trouble which would cause her to throw herself overboard. She was last seen on deck early in the evening, and went below a little after nine. A remarkable coincidence is that her cabin adjoined that of Mr. Cornelius Patterson, from which the jewel was stolen; but whether there is any connection between the two is not known.' "

"There, gentlemen, what do you think of that?" asked the commander, laying down the wireless and looking down the table. "Come, Blake, this is in your line. What do you think of it?"

But Sexton Blake did not answer. He was sitting with furrowed brow, in deep thought. It had flashed across him while the commander was reading that the jewel which had been stolen during the night on the Mastodonic was called the "Sun's Eye." From that his mind leaped to the frivolous message carried by the homing pigeon. Where had it come from? What was the meaning of that message? That it had some connection with the theft he had now no doubt, and so strangely had it been drawn into the mystery, that he had more than an ordinary interest in the matter.

Above all, did the missing Miss Ford have any connection with the theft? It did not seem reasonable. If anyone disappeared from a ship in mid-ocean, with no other craft about, it seemed a certainty that they could only go to the bottom. No. It was probably pure coincidence. And Lieutenant Bruce was voicing almost that very thought in replying to the commander's remark.

"I don't see, sir, how the missing girl could have any connection with the theft. If she is not on board the Mastodonic, she must be in the sea. And surely, even if she were insane, she wouldn't steal the jewel, only to jump overboard with it."

The commander smiled.

"Always the ladies' champion, lieutenant. But, come, Blake! You seem wrapped in mystery. Does your deductive mind see further than ours?"

Blake looked up.

"I don't know, commander," he said slowly. "In a certain way, this has come as a bit of a shock to me, for it just happens to come on top of a most remarkable thing which happened during the night on our way out."

All eyes turned to Blake, intense interest written in them.

"Is it something which you can tell us, Blake?" asked the commander.

"Certainly!" answered Blake. "But before doing so, I will ask you all to please consider it confidential. I have a half-formed plan in my mind, and if I put it into execution I would not care for any publicity."

Commander Villiers turned to a steward who stood near the door.

"Retire, Smith, and close the door. Now, Blake, I can answer for the discretion of myself and my officers."

"And for mine," put in Whitcomb.

Blake lit a fresh cigar, and leaned back.

"Well, commander, and gentlemen, if I begin by telling you that during the night I ran into a homing pigeon bound landwards, you will see that what I speak of is rather remarkable."

Then, with that vivid detail which seemed a part of him, Blake recounted the story of the pigeon and the note it carried. A breathless interest followed him until he reached the point where he had read the note.

"As you know," he said, "the name of the jewel which was stolen from the Mastodonic was the 'Sun's Eye.' This is what was in the note: 'What price Sun's Eye?' Nothing more. I have the note in my map-holder, and the wounded pigeon in the grub-locker."

A gasp of astonishment went around the table.

"By Jove, Blake, that is one of the most remarkable coincidences I ever heard!" exclaimed the commander. "For whom do you suppose the note was really intended?"

"I haven't the remotest idea. If we knew, I imagine it would throw some light on this extraordinary occurrence."

"It almost seems as though you ought to follow it up, Mr. Blake," remarked Lieutenant Bruce.

"That was just what I was thinking," replied Blake. "It certainly presents some interesting points."

"But how would you go ahead?" asked the commander.

"How far away is the Mastodonic from here?" countered Blake.

"Between eighty and a hundred miles. You surely don't intend—"

"Exactly," interrupted Blake, smiling. "Since we have been talking I have decided. The Grey Panther is able to make that in a short time, and I can overtake the Mastodonic. If you will send a private wireless to the captain, and, tell him I am coming, he will have time to rig up a landing-float of some kind. But I would tell him to keep it secret. Then I can look into matters without being bothered. I'm afraid, Whitcomb, you will have to start homewards alone."

"By Jove, I'll wait here until we get a wireless from you!" laughed Whitcomb. "The interest in this thing has swamped my interest in the race."

"I'll do everything I can for you, Blake," remarked the commander. "I'll fix up a wireless to Captain Brown, and get him to rig up a landing-platform for you. I'm in the same position as Whitcomb. If you really overtake the Mastodonic, send us wireless, or, better still, stop off here on your way back. We'll be at fever-pitch to hear what you discover."

"Thanks, commander!" laughed Blake. "I will stop off here on my way back. I really intend going, and the sooner I start the better."

Commander Villiers rose, and a minute later they were all

congregated on the landing-platform. The engineer's assistant lifted out the wounded homing pigeon, which was passed round, and then Blake showed them the note which had been attached to its leg.

"It's simply marvellous,!" remarked the commander again and again.

Blake, at the commander's suggestion, turned the pigeon over to the care of the ship's surgeon, until his return, and, sending a sailor for Tinker, began getting into his flying-togs. Tinker, with the middies surrounding him, came up, with a look of wonder on his face.

"What is it, guv'nor? Are we returning already?"

"No. We are going to make a test flight from here to the Mastodonic," jerked Blake briefly.

Tinker was devoured with curiosity; but he had been trained to instant obedience as well as the midshipmen about him, and, without further remark, reached for his flying-togs.

They wheeled out the Grey Panther, and headed her towards the side. Then Blake climbed in. But Tinker turned to shake hands with his new friends.

"We're coming back here," said Blake. "Come my lad!"

Tinker dropped his hand and climbed in, and while two sailors held the graceful grey shape, Whitcomb started the engine. He signed to them to release her, and she shot towards the side. For a bare moment she hovered over the water after leaving the platform, but as Blake canted the wings she soared upwards in a wide turn.

Tinker waved his hand to the tiny dots already far below, and settled down as Blake, hunched over the wheel in deep thought, with his eyes on the compass, headed for the track of the Mastodonic.

In the light of the blue flares Yvonne waited.

Blake volplaned straight for the stern.

A vivid flash of lightning revealed the land close at hand

CAPTAIN BROWN, commander of the Mastodonic, and commodore of the Northern Star Line, sat in his chart-room chewing the end of a cold cigar and frowning over a brief wireless message which had just been handed to him.

It was, to say the least, rather startling to be informed that an aeroplane would board him at sea, and that fact, together with the wireless advice, was certainly a radical advance over the old windjammer days when he had received his first initiation into the mysteries and hardships of navigation.

But Captain Brown was not in command of the most luxurious floating palace without having earned his position, and no man living could have fulfilled the responsibility and duty with more suavity blended with decision. If he accepted the words of the wireless message as fact, it meant that Sexton Blake in an aeroplane would make his appearance out of the sky in something under two hours, and there would not be more than enough time to erect a landing-platform.

On the other hand, it meant the Mastodonic must be slowed down to half speed, and Captain Brown saw his hoped-for maiden record going by the boards. Had it been the robbery of the "Sun's Eye" alone he would have kept straight on and left the discovery of it to the ship's detectives, but a missing passenger was no light matter.

If Sexton Blake could throw any light on the matter it would be a great relief. Besides, Cornelius Patterson was making no bones about connecting the disappearance of the great jewel with the missing Miss Ford, and that was bad for the ship.

No; the record must be given up this trip, and everything possible done to clear the matter up. As he made his decision Captain Brown stuffed the wireless message into his pocket and betook himself to the bridge. He sent a man for the purser and the wireless operator, and then retired again to the chart-room, where he wrote busily for a few moments.

The purser was the first to appear, and as he stood and saluted the captain looked up.

"You might copy this notice out and post if about on all the notice-boards, Mr. Baily," he said briefly. "Also have it inserted in the ship's papers."

"Very good, sir," replied the purser. His brows went up in astonishment as he read what the captain had written, but he made no remark as he hurried himself away to post up several copies.

Half an hour later every notice-board on the ship carried the following notice:

"NOTICE.

"The captain of the Mastodonic has been informed by wireless that an aeroplane will land on the ship during the day. A landing-platform will be put up over the stern, but no passengers will be admitted to the deck for the present. Later, before the departure of the aviator, a full opportunity will be given to inspect the machine.

"BY ORDER."

The wireless operator was the next to put in an appearance, and after writing out an answer to Commander Villiers of the Thor, Captain Brown warned him to keep the coming aviator's identity a secret, and then sent for the fourth officer.

That individual was soon busy with a gang of sailors erecting the landing-platform. Several iron stanchions were put up, and with the true ingenuity of the sailor a large stretch of canvas was dragged to the scene of operations. Stretching and pulling, with many lusty yells, they soon had a sound if yielding platform fixed up, and stretching clear across the stern.

Another hour of anticipation went by before the look-out sighted a black speck on the horizon, which rapidly grew until it achieved the proportions of a bird. On and on it came, and when the glasses showed it to be the expected 'plane a wild rush was made on every deck to witness the approach.

Under the fourth officer the gang of sailors on the hastily-improvised landing-deck stood by to receive the 'plane. Every eye was glued to the long, graceful lines of the speeding grey shape, and as the hum of the Gnome reached their ears, and then stopped for the volplane, Captain Brown signalled the engine-room the "full stop."

The great mammoth liner forged slowly ahead under the force of her former impetus, but Blake, high up, was judging her speed with careful eye.

Slowly he swung round until he was astern, but planing in the same direction. Then, slightly dipping the nose of the Grey Panther, he volplaned straight for the stern. Every breath was drawn in sharply as he disappeared from the view of those on the lower deck, but up above the wheels of the chassis had bit the yielding surface of the stretched canvas, and had run forward to stop in the centre in a magnificent landing.

Captain Brown received Blake, who climbed stiffly out, and, signing to Tinker to follow, still goggled, he followed die captain to the chart-room.

"Well, Mr. Blake," remarked the captain, as he closed the door and waved Tinker into a chair, while Blake divested himself of his goggles and cap, "I must confess Commander Villiers message gave me a great surprise. It is odd that you should have been on the Thor. But let me give you and your young companion some refreshment."

"The wireless operator of the Thor picked up your message, and as the matter is of more than ordinary interest to me I came on in the machine," replied Blake, as the captain rang for a steward. "I'd like to investigate the loss of the jewel and the disappearance of your lady passenger."

"Certainly you are welcome to do so, Mr. Blake! The matter is in the hands of the ship's detectives, but when I heard you were coming I was glad, for it is an easy matter to conceal a small jewel on a ship like this with so many passengers, and of course it is impossible to make an individual search. I wouldn't mind that so much, for it is liable to happen on any ship, but in forty years I have never lost a passenger, and I am more than puzzled over the sudden disappearance of Miss Ford."

"Ah! Well, the first thing to do, captain, is to keep my identity a secret. Then if you can supply me with an officer's uniform as a disguise, and come with me, I would like to make a thorough examination of Cornelius Patterson's cabin and also that of the missing lady. Then I can ask any questions that occur, and get away again without causing you too much delay. There will be no objection to the examination, I suppose?"

"Oh, no; I guess not. The ship's detectives have already made one, but I will send for Mr. Patterson, and he can accompany us."

Captain Brown rang, and sent for the Canadian millionaire.

"Oh, Mr. Patterson," he said, as the millionaire entered, "have you any objection to one of my officers making another examination of your cabin?"

"None at all," replied Patterson. "All I want to do is to recover my jewel; but my opinion is it won't be found until the missing woman is found."

This was pure bluff on Patterson's part, for he thought the "Sun's Eye" safe by now in the hands of his accomplice in England.

The disappearance of the lady who occupied the adjoining cabin had been seized upon by him as a remarkably lucky coincidence, and he had lost no time in hinting that she could probably inform them as to the whereabouts of his property. It is not hard to imagine his chagrin had he known that all unknowingly he had hit on the truth, and instead of the "Sun's Eye" travelling gaily by pigeon post to England it was even then in the possession of his fair neighbour who had so mysteriously disappeared.

Blake, while waiting for Patterson's arrival in the chart-room, had himself got into an officer's uniform and procured a middy's uniform for Tinker.

Consequently, Patterson never dreamed that the officer and midshipman who accompanied Captain Brown to his cabin were the two who had just landed in the aeroplane, and that their identity was that of the greatest detective living and his assistant.

But even had he known he would not have objected to another examination, so sure of himself did he feel.

Blake closed the door on entering the cabin, and turned at once to the millionaire.

"Do you mind showing me the trunk or box from which your jewel was stolen, Mr. Patterson?"

"Not at all," he replied.

Leaning down, he pulled out a black steamer trunk from under the bunk, and unlocked it.

"There it is. That cashbox in the corner was where I put the jewel before retiring, and you can see for yourself, neither its lock nor that of the trunk bear the slightest marks of violence."

Blake picked up the cashbox, and made a close examination of the lock of the trunk, but what Patterson had said was true. They bore not the slightest sign of having been forced.

As Blake bent down to replace the cashbox in the corner of the trunk, his eye caught something which seemed to cause him some interest, for he bent closer and pretended to again examine the cashbox.

"Do you always have a couple of holes in the back of your trunk, Mr. Patterson?" he asked, casually straightening up.

For a bare moment Patterson hesitated, but so brief was it that Blake was the only one to notice it.

"Oh—er—no, not always," he said, in as careless a tone as Blake's. "That trunk has holes owing to the fact that I brought it home from the West Indies, filled with cigars, and desired to prevent them from getting too dry."

Which was a very reasonable explanation, and one which Blake seemed to accept, for he nodded, and said no more. But something else had caught Blake's eye in the bottom of the cabin trunk, and of this he made no mention. But it told him that Cornelius Patterson was lying.

What he saw was two small bits of grain such as is used for bird food, and more than anything else that told him he had found the originating source of the homing pigeon's strange journey. But what of the seemingly frivolous note which it had carried? He could see absolutely no meaning in it, and with wrinkled brow he turned and said shortly:

"I'd like to look at the cabin of the missing passenger, captain. That will be all here, thank you, Mr. Patterson."

They were just turning to go out, when the wireless operator entered with a message for Cornelius Patterson. With an apology, he tore it open, and, accustomed as he was to control his features, the closely-watching Blake saw his face pale and his hand shake ever so slightly as his eyes remained glued on the words.

"No bad news, I hope, Mr. Patterson," remarked Blake suavely.

Patterson came to himself with a jerk.

"Er— no—no!" he said hastily. "But if you will excuse me, gentlemen, I will go up and send a reply. It's a matter of business which must be attended to at once."

He departed hastily, and Captain Brown led the way into the cabin of the missing Miss Ford.

Blake first made an examination of the sleeping cabin. Beyond a trunk and a bag, however, there was no luggage, and his closest scrutiny of their contents failed to reveal the slightest thing beyond some very fine and very dainty, feminine garments.

He then led the way to the outer cabin, and examined the trunk under the couch and the black bag. They, like the luggage inside, revealed nothing, and, signing to the captain to lock the door, he pulled out his glass and dropped to his knees.

First tackling the partition between the cabin they were in and that of Cornelius Patterson, Blake began a minute examination. Up and down over and across he went, covering the area in dozens of tiny imaginary squares, which took in every tiny speck on the white wall. For half an hour he worked in silence, while Tinker followed him with his eyes, and Captain Brown stood looking on in wonderment. But at the end of that time Blake paused in his survey, and concentrated his attention on the line where two of the panels joined.

"Go into the next cabin, Tinker," he said, "and come close to the wall on the other side of where I am."

Tinker hurried out, and a moment later his voice came from Patterson's cabin.

"Is this right, guv'nor?"

"No —a little more to your left."

"How's this?"

"That's right. Now watch carefully where the panels join."

Blake reached in his pocket as he spoke, and drew out a tiny, slim, steel instrument. He thrust the point in the small hole he had discovered, and pushed it through until he judged the point to be on the other side.

"Can you see anything where they join?" he called.

"No, guv'nor; but there's a bunk here, you know."

"Look underneath it then!" snapped Blake. "If it's dark, run your finger up and down the wall."

For a moment there was silence, then —

"Oh! I should say there was something! I've run something sharp into my finger!"

Blake smiled grimly.

"Just wait a moment, captain. I want to see where this goes through."

He hastened into Patterson's cabin, and looked underneath the bunk where the steel point came through. Then with Tinker following, he returned to the other cabin and proceeded to go through a mysterious course of actions. First he rang for a steward and requested the man to bring a long piece of rope. While he waited, he took off his shoes and stood up on the couch. When the man returned, he tied the rope under his arms, and squeezed with difficulty through the porthole, and Tinker and the captain lowered him slowly. When his eyes were about three feet below the porthole, he called to them to stop, and, pulling himself in close, began examining a mark which he saw on the white paint. From his pocket he drew a delicate mould, and took an impression of the mark; then, signalling to the captain and Tinker, he worked his way up and back through the port.

"What on earth did you go out there for?" asked Captain Brown, in amazement.

Blake laughed.

"I'll explain later. A certain theory has been forming in my head; it suggested an examination of the outside under the porthole. And now, captain, let us return to the chart-room. I wish to ask some questions."

On their arrival Blake went straight to the point.

"Firstly, captain, can you give me a detailed description of the missing Miss Ford?"

"I certainly can," replied the captain energetically. "She wasn't aboard long, but, by James, Sir, there never was a better conducted young lady in the world. She was one of the most beautiful girls I ever saw. Medium height, slim and perfect features. One of those women that made a man feel sort of protective towards her at once."

"Your description is enthusiastic enough." smiled Blake drily, "but I'm afraid hardly of much use for my purpose. Perhaps I had better ask you a few questions. You say she was of medium height?"

"Yes, about five feet five."

"What colour was her hair?"

"The most beautiful shade of bronze you can imagine. Tons of it, too."

"Ah!" said Blake sharply. "And her eyes?"

"Blue-blue as the bluest sea."

"I don't need to ask about her dress," went on Blake. "I can judge that from the luggage in her cabin. How about jewellery? Did she wear much? Anything distinctive?"

"No; on the contrary, she wore hardly any. Usually just a big Egyptian scarab on her left hand."

Blake leaned forward.

"Are you positive of that fact?" he asked.

Captain Brown nodded.

"Certainly. I noticed it when she came up on the bridge before sailing, and again when chatting with her in the restaurant. In fact, I remarked on it, and she told me she got it in Egypt."

"Can you arrange that I see a copy of the wireless message which Mr. Patterson received in the cabin, and a copy of his reply?"

"It's against the regulations, but I'll arrange it. Will you wait here, and I will myself bring a copy of each?"

"What do you make of it, guv'nor?" asked Tinker, as the captain left.

"I don't yet know, my lad," replied Blake. "It's baffling, but I am going to try to make arrangements to leave you here, and I'll navigate the 'plane alone. I want you to follow Cornelius Patterson wherever he goes. I think that gentleman knows more about the disappearance of the Sun's Eye than he appears to. So does Yvonne."

"What, guv'nor! You don't mean to say—"

At that moment the captain returned with the copies of the wireless messages, and Blake spread them out on the table. The one which Patterson had received was very brief, and would convey no meaning to the uninitiated. It originated from a place in Surrey, and read simply: "Groundless not received yet. Was it sent?"

But Blake read "groundless" as referring to nothing more likely than something not dependent upon the ground, and what more logical in view of what he already knew than the homing-pigeon? The next was a trifle longer, and was addressed to:

"Brown, Horton, Surrey.—Groundless arranged. Sent positively. Investigate thoroughly. Advise."

For several minutes Blake studied the two messages, and then he turned to Captain Brown.

"Captain," he said, "I think I can state that your missing passenger, Miss Ford, is not at the bottom of the sea; also, that the jewel missing from Mr. Patterson's trunk is not on the ship. These two messages clear up the points which were missing in my theory, but I am very sorry that I cannot tell you more now. Will you leave the matter in my hands, and trust to me to clear it up? I am afraid I can tell you nothing definite until you return to England on your homeward trip."

"I am very anxious to clear matters up, Mr. Blake; but if you are quite positive Miss Ford is not drowned, and that there is a chance of recovering Mr. Patterson's property, of course I'll wait. But I can't imagine how she could have disappeared."

"How did I arrive, captain?" asked Blake quietly.

"Good heavens, do you mean to say—"

"Steady, captain; you must have patience!" smiled Blake. "What I want to do is to leave my assistant on board to follow up a clue. Will that be satisfactory to you?"

"Yes; if you wish."

"Very well; he can keep on that uniform, and pose as a midshipman. He may possibly return with you, and I wouldn't be surprised if you had another passenger returning with you —Mr. Patterson."

Disregarding the captain's astonished look, Blake rose.

"If the passengers want to have a look at the machine, they had better go up now," he remarked. "I'll go into the restaurant and get something to eat, and then get away. Come, Tinker, I will give you your instructions while we lunch."

Tinker followed Blake to the restaurant while the captain permitted the passengers a hurried view of the aeroplane.

Then as he saw Blake approaching, his features concealed in cap and goggles, he waved the last curious one below, and ordered the sailors to wheel out the Grey Panther. Blake climbed in, and five minutes later shot over the side, and, to the accompaniment of the passengers' cheers and a long, deep blast of the Mastodon's syren, he circled and rose, putting the 'plane ahead on its journey, of which the super-Dreadnought was to be a landing-stage.

The Fifth Chapter.   The Race with the Hurricane —Blake Deduces.

BLAKE had a battling journey from the Thor to Hendon. He had landed on the super-Dreadnought after a clinking trip from the Mastodonic, and found his good-natural rival Whitcomb smoking and kicking his heels in patience until Blake's return.

Blake told the interested officers of the Thor as much as he thought wise of his discoveries, and, after watching Whitcomb get away with a good start for Hendon, he began preparing for his own return journey.

The ship's surgeon had discovered the homing-pigeon to be not badly injured, prophesying that it would fly with its former vigour in a day or two.

In compliance with the passenger condition of the test flight, Blake borrowed a delighted midshipman from Commander Villiers, the only difficulty being to decide which one.

Every middy on the Thor applied, and so pressing were their each and every argument to be taken, that Blake settled the matter by drawing lots.

The youngster to whom the choice fell was a bright lad about Tinker's size, and, after packing the pigeon in the grub locker, Blake made hurried farewells and got away. Whitcomb was already long out of sight, putting the reliable Farman to her pace in his endeavour to win the test.

On the first part of the journey back, after the middy had got over his first taste of being high up and driving along at over eighty miles an hour, Blake explained, the details of aeroplaning.

The grey hulk of the Thor had dropped behind, and but for the presence of a brig under full sail far below, sea and sky were empty of life besides themselves.

For a full two hours they drove along, but failed to sight the Farman.

A lowering of the sky in the west caused Blake to look at the barometer. He was amazed at its sudden drop, and, swinging round the storm-mirror, gazed frowningly at the reflection therein of the western sky.

"We're in for a bad blow, my lad!" he shouted. "It's following us up, but unless it's going a hundred miles an hour we'll beat it yet!"

The middy nodded. Young as he was, a season on the China station had inured him to sudden storms, and the elements had no terrors for him. He swung the barometer around, and squinted at it in a comical imitation of Commander Villiers.

"Aye'll get it all right, sir!" he shouted. "It's coming after us pretty sharp!"

Blake nodded, and tightened the storm stays. Carter, the middy, true to his sea-training, dug around and found the waterproof which covered the chart-stand. To the accompaniment of Blake's approving smile, he fastened it on, and then turned on the searchlight.

As far as possible, the frail little aeroplane was now storm-ready, and Blake settled into his seat.

Even through the noise of the engine and the whir of the propeller they could feel a deadness in the air. Although it rushed past them at a tremendous pace, its life seemed gone like the stirring of dust in a giant vacuum.

Blake watched the west in the mirror before him. The ever-growing blackness was climbing behind them to the zenith like a black, sinister hand ready to pounce down on the ships on the tossing waves far below and the bold grey shape which raced through the air.

The brig, a mere dot on the horizon, had stripped to bare poles. Carter picked up the glasses, and watched her as the hurricane struck and heeled her over.

"It's got the brig!" he shouted. "It will hit us in a few minutes! Must be travelling at a quick rate!"

Blake nodded, but before he could reply, and even through the noise of the machine, came a faint moaning sound, which grew and grew until it dominated and swallowed everything else.

Driving as they were at over eighty miles, it overtook them with its fury, and, had they been flying in its teeth, the Grey Panther would not have lived a second. Darkness spread with marvellous rapidity as the giant black cloud leaped over the sky.

Below, the waves were being whipped to a frenzy of white, and then came the first blinding flash of lightning, accompanied by a terrific crack of thunder.

The gale was upon them in its full fury!

The Grey Panther was doing her very best. Did she falter now, it would be a hopeless race. Spurred on by the hurricane, Blake sent her on with every ounce of speed the whirling Gnome could muster. But still the flame of lightning in the rear seemed to grow and grow until it threatened to engulf the little aeroplane and her two intrepid occupants in its scorching maw.

Whether it had overtaken Whitcomb, Blake did not know; but that ever-approaching lightning cloud behind was spur enough to make fast time without thinking of the race itself.

In the light of a particularly brilliant flash Blake sighted land, and, throwing the chart-lamp on the compass, set his course for Hendon. A driving rain overtook them then, threatening in its fury to beat them to earth. Carter twisted around, and swept the searchlight ahead, but it was really the lightning which eventually showed them Hendon.

Shutting off the engine, Blake volplaned to the enclosure, and was met by the news that Whitcomb had not yet arrived. It transpired later that the storm had forced him to ground a bare hour out of Hendon, and once again the papers rang with the triumph of Blake and the Grey Panther. It seemed a foregone conclusion that the staunch little machine should tackle the final test of the meeting— the race from Hendon to Paris and back.

Blake didn't look for any further developments of any importance in the mystery which he had so oddly become mixed up in until Tinker reported from New York. He decided to take Carter as passenger on the Hendon-Paris race, and with that end in view installed the delighted youngster in Tinker's room at Baker Street. He then set out for the City, where he spent a profitable morning around the insurance offices, for he discovered there that Cornelius Patterson had insured the Sun's Eye against theft for half a million, paying a substantial premium for the cover. Part of the mystery Blake could now reconstruct, and as he sat hunched up in his chair in the consulting-room that night, he went over the points one by one.

"It is Yvonne! I am sure of it!" he muttered. "It bears her stamp in every point. But Patterson himself is a crook. I wonder if she knew that when she succeeded in getting possession of the jewel? But how on earth did she manage it? A homing-pigeon collides with the aeroplane at night over mid ocean. We find a most frivolous note attached to it which refers to the Sun's Eye. Then the next morning we hear that the Sun's Eye has been stolen from its owner in mid ocean, and on the top of that comes the news of the mysterious disappearance of a lady passenger. Patterson lied when he said those two holes in his trunk were for permitting air to circulate when bringing cigars in it from the West Indies.

"I'll stake anything it was the first time the trunk had ever been used. Then those two grains of bird food. That proves the homing-pigeon was kept secretly in the trunk, and the holes were to provide it with air when the trunk was closed.

"Then I discover the Sun's Eye was insured for half a million against theft. From that, if mathematical deduction be correct, it would seem a certainty that Patterson robbed himself, and sent the jewel by the homing-pigeon to a confederate in England. I must find that confederate, and I think when Master Pigeon is well enough to fly, I can use him for the purpose.

"Then there is that tiny hole between the cabin of the missing lady and Patterson's. In view of the possible identity of that passenger, I think it quite likely that mademoiselle kept herself informed of her neighbour's movements by a sound magnifier. The Mastodonic is on her maiden trip, and mademoiselle was the first occupant of that cabin. Consequently, it was safe to assume that the hole was made by her own charming self.

"Next, how did she get hold of the pigeon? Patterson would release it probably at night, and the chances are through the porthole. If she was aware of this and acted sharp, she might be able to intercept it; but if your ingenuity really has accomplished that, mademoiselle, I bow to you.

"At any rate, I'm certain Patterson didn't write the note which I found on the pigeon. Proof that the bird passed through someone else's hands after leaving him. Then there was his agitation on receiving that wireless from Surrey and his reply. If 'groundless' didn't refer to the pigeon, I'll be very much astonished. No wonder his accomplice is worrying about the bird's non-appearance. At any rate, I'll take the bird to Horton in Surrey, and follow it home. Patterson's accomplice will wire him to New York, that the bird hasn't arrived, and I'll wager Patterson comes back to Europe hot-foot to investigate. They will look sick when the pigeon turns up a fortnight late.

"But by the terms of the insurance contract, the company will have to pay up the half million if the stone is not recovered. Patterson deserved to lose it to mademoiselle's superior cleverness, but since the company has authorised me to-day to go ahead on it, I'm afraid, mademoiselle, it will be an interesting chase to outgeneral you and regain it. I'll attend to Patterson's case, too. I really must caution you, mademoiselle, to leave off wearing that scarab, although I really believe Captain Brown's fervent description of your hair and eyes would have told me who the missing lady passenger was. It will be interesting to hear from your own lips the story of how you managed to leave the Mastodonic at sea.

"But if I'm going to tackle that race to-morrow I'd better get some sleep. Plucky little chap, Carter, but I wish it had been possible to have had Tinker."

Blake went to bed that night with a strange elation filling him, but he would not admit even to himself that it was caused by the thought that the coming days might bring him once more face to face with that perverse yet altogether lovable girl, who held such an unrealised place in his life, and who through all her wanderings and exploits wore next her heart a tiny miniature of the man who for her loomed head and shoulders over all others—Sexton Blake.

The Sixth Chapter. The Hendon-Paris Race— Sexton Blake Sees An Old Friend.

"ARE you really determined on taking part in the Hendon-Paris race, Yvonne?"

It was Graves speaking, and he stood under a big spreading elm on the lawn of a beautiful old Tudor country house in Surrey. Centuries had elapsed since the stately stone pile had been reared to form a fitting home for the son and heir of a hard-fighting baron. The trees and soft yielding turf reflected the dignity and beauty of the mansion which they set off, and not least fitting and harmonious was the charming, bronze-haired girl, who lay back gracefully in a long, low chair on the lawn, the sun dancing distractingly through her hair as it shot its ardent spears between the tangled branches and leaves of the giant elm.

By her side was a small wicker table, heaped with magazines and, let me whisper it, sweets. The solemn old butler, who had passed to Yvonne with the mansion, gazed with cold eye on his young mistress's weakness, and little did he dream that the dainty, charming girl who ruled so imperiously yet kindly, was that much famed and much sought after —by Scotland Yard —Mademoiselle Yvonne.

After her daring escapade on the Mastodonic, Yvonne, always whimsical, had gone down to Surrey to the old mansion which she had bought, there to revel in the things which really appealed to her. Over and over again had she pictured herself walking back and forth under that shady, dignified elm walk for which the place was famous; and over and over again she had pictured as her companion Sexton Blake.

She feared it could never be, but love always hopes, and strange though she was, Yvonne's heart was very girlish and very feminine. That he was using the powder of his brilliant mind to discover the whereabouts of the Sun's Eye, Yvonne hadn't the remotest suspicion. She thought the thing still a complete mystery, and laughed with delicious enjoyment as she thought of Cornelius Patterson's discomfiture and Captain Brown's mystification.

Her agents in America would advise her when Patterson reached home, and then she would send him a brief communication informing him that the loss of the Sun's Eye was his share of the debt contracted long ago in sunny Australia. The birds and the grass, the fields and the trees, in all their summer softness and splendour, appealed to her, and she would for the present put everything else aside. Her life was not too happy, and the old Surrey place formed a charming retreat.

She glanced up lazily as her uncle asked the question. "Why, yes, uncle, I think so. Any objection?"

"Little good it would do if I had," drawled Graves, who was lounging about in keen enjoyment in a well-fitting flannel suit. "You know it's dangerous, Yvonne. Suppose you were recognised?—Scotland Yard would have the drag-net out for you in an hour."

Yvonne laughed.

"Don't worry, uncle. They won't recognise me. I have a particular reason for taking part in the race. Have you read this morning's paper?"

"Yes, why?"

"Well, then, you must have seen that Sexton Blake is in the race. The papers have been full of nothing else but his exploits with that monoplane of his. I've an idea that my own Silverwings can beat his, and I can imagine nothing better than racing Blake to Paris and back."

"But the entry," protested Graves. "They will investigate each participator, and you know the risk."

"Oh, I am not going to enter!" smiled Yvonne, lighting the tiny cigarette. "I'll fly about on a higher level over Hendon until the race starts, and then I'll join in. On the return I'll finish over Hendon, and keep right on to here.

"Silverwings is absolutely invisible five hundred feet from the ground. Only the competitors can see me, and then only when they are in the air. They will be surprised, of course; but during the race they will be too busy, and after they finish they won't know where I've gone to. I'll put on goggles so they won't recognise me. By the way, uncle, what time is it?"

"Just gone eleven."

"You might give orders to have the machine got ready. I will leave here at twelve, in order to be over Hendon in plenty of time."

•　　•　　•　　•　　•

Sexton Blake wheeled the Grey Panther out of the hangar at Hendon, and made a last examination of wings, stays, and engine before leaving on the Hendon-Paris race, which was to be more than anything else, a speed test.

Lennox, in a Bleriot, had got away at one o'clock, while

Whitcomb had limped into Hendon with his Farman that morning, disappointed, but determined to make another try for a record. He was just leaving as Blake walked across the ground, and the great detective joined the crowd in a hearty send off.

Then he climbed into his own machine, and, with young Carter in Tinker's seat, started the engine. Making a preliminary low flight, he came back to the ground, in order to give Whitcomb half an hour's start. Then, once more sending the Gnome engine whirling, the Grey Panther shot in the air, and headed for Paris.

During the first few minutes Blake was too occupied in getting the engine warmed up, and watching how the Grey Panther shaped, to notice anything else. On rising he had, as is usual with the pilot, cast his glance around the horizon, but Whitcomb had already disappeared, and, of course, Lennox was well on his way. As he finished his inspection, however, and swung the mirror around facing him, he glanced up, and was puzzled at the look in Carter's face.

"What is it?" shouted Blake.

"I —I don't know exactly," replied Carter. "I thought for a moment that I had seen another aeroplane behind us, but it shot up so quickly I'm not sure."

"I hardly think it possible," shouted Blake. "We are the last to start, and there are no other competitors."

"But it didn't look like any machine I have ever seen," persisted the lad. "It was silver-blue, and seemed to melt into the atmosphere."

"I am afraid you are getting airman's false eye," called Blake, smiling, but the smile quickly passed as his eyes fell on the mirror before him.

There the blue sky had been mirrored with only the reflection of delicate sky to spoil its azure depths. But now, as he looked, from the very centre of the blue seemed to appear a vague silver line, which grew until it took the form of a giant bird, and then that of an aeroplane. But what, an aeroplane! Gigantic as compared to the slim lines of the Grey Panther, its great wings stretching out in lines of silver.

It was indeed well-named by Yvonne —Silverwings.

Blake looked up and spoke.

"You were right, after all, my lad, but I can't imagine whose it can be. I know they claim to have machines in France, and also in Germany, which are invisible a short distance from the ground, and I wouldn't surprised if this is one of them. I'm going to send the Grey Panther for all she is worth. Watch our friends behind, and see if they follow. It may be a foreign machine, surreptitiously watching our tests."

Carter nodded excitedly, and kept his eyes glued on the great machine which was coming on above and behind at a pace which threatened to overhaul them before they got over the Channel. From time to time he shouted out its progress to Blake, who, hunched over the steering-gear, was sending the Grey Panther along at a pace equal to that which they had achieved in their thrilling race with the gale.

At last a sparkling sunlit streak appeared. It grew and grew in width until the land dropped suddenly behind, and they were over the Channel. Up to now the mysterious machine following them had kept at a uniform distance, but as the Grey Panther ate up the miles between England and France, the great silver body shot past them, and the Grey Panther tipped and rocked ominously in her back draught.

"Whoever is driving it is a good sport, anyway, shouted the lad, as the other machine, seeing the danger its back draught had caused, shot up to a higher level.

Then the Grey Panther leaped forward again, and neck and neck the two 'planes shot forward over French soil, leaving the Channel a rapidly-diminishing streak behind them.

At that moment Lennox, in his Bleriot, raced past on the return journey, but the driver of the strange machine had evidently spotted him in the distance. By the time he had passed Blake, the detective's mysterious competitor had disappeared far above, and not until Lennox had dwindled to a dark speck did it descend again.

Rapidly the country unfolded beneath them like a mammoth map, and soon after passing Lennox, they sighted Whitcomb on his Farman. Again the strange machine shot up out of sight, but when Paris appeared like a tumbled mass of soiled chalk beneath them, it once more dropped, and, still racing neck and neck, they headed for the towering, graceful lace-like lines of the Eiffel Tower.

"Whoever it is, they didn't want Lennox or Whitcomb to see them," muttered Blake. "I wonder what their object is? Is it possible they know I am driving this machine, and are making a personal race with me? If that is what they want, by thunder, they will get it! With the wind behind us going back, I think the Grey Panther will do herself justice."

Blake turned the wheel, and the right-hand wing shot up as the Grey Panther banked in a short, dangerous, but second-saving circle round Eiffel Tower, where the judge dropped a flag to signify that the condition had been satisfactorily complied with. By wireless from Hendon he had been advised that only three machines were in the race, and he must have rubbed his eyes with astonishment as the giant silver-blue shape of Blake's competitor flashed past after the Grey Panther.

In this fashion they tore back on their return trip—Blake grim and determined, and his unknown competitor evidently no less so. There was very little to choose between them. Over the Channel, the big machine held the lead, but as the water shot behind, the Grey Panther gained once more, pulling up steadily. As they drew nearer Hendon, Blake knit his brows in puzzlement as he saw his mysterious competitor drop to the thousand-foot level on which the Grey Panther was flying, and draw steadily nearer and nearer.

"Now, what does he want?" muttered Blake. "If he keeps on that course, we'll be crashing into each other."

What the other wanted, however, was not long in doubt. Barely two hundred yards now separated them, and, as far as he dared, Blake was giving his attention to the powerful lines of the other machine. Up in the cockpit, he could just see the head and shoulders of the other driver. He riveted his gaze there as he saw one hand reach up and tear off cap and goggles.

Then Blake gazed in stupefaction at what he saw, and so surprised was he that the Grey Panther swerved dangerously as his hand relaxed. Over the edge of the other machine he could see the sun glancing off the heavy bronze coils of a woman's hair. He needed no more to tell him the identity of his mysterious competitor, but he smiled a grim smile as Yvonne turned around and laughed at him, waving her free hand as she did so.

Blake waved his hand in reply, and for a moment he was tempted to keep straight on after the other machine. Hendon swept in view at that moment, and before Blake had time to decide, Yvonne with another laugh and wave, sent her machine high up, to be lost a moment later in the deep blue above.

"That settles it," muttered Blake. "I might search the sky all day, and never pick her up again. What a machine, though! Its colour is ideal for the purpose, blending, as it does, with the colour of the sky. But wait, mademoiselle; I'll locate you yet."

He had no more time then for anything but the machine, for Hendon was below, and, with a last glance into the unfathomable blue sky, where Yvonne had disappeared, Blake volplaned down to ground, to be greeted with thunderous applause. He had beaten Lennox and Whitcomb in the great race, and through every test the Grey Panther had passed supreme.

"But not supreme,'' muttered Blake, as he walked wearily into his rooms that night. "Yvonne has as much speed, and I think I will change the colour of the Grey Panther to silver blue. And now that the flying is over, mademoiselle, I will have time to look more thoroughly into the matter of the Sun's Eye, and perhaps—perhaps we will meet again."

YVONNE

The Seventh Chapter. Tinker on a Long Chase —A Suspicious Quarry.

TINKER'S instincts rebelled at being left on the Mastodonic, on a seemingly tame mission, while Blake departed in the Grey Panther without him; but he realised with a sigh that duty was duty, and since he had to stay he might as well find out as much about Mr. Cornelius Patterson as possible. At his suggestion, Captain Brown installed him in the cabin which had been occupied by the missing Miss Ford, and Tinker grinned to himself as he found himself in the atmosphere created by Yvonne's remaining belongings.

"I can't see through as much as the guv'nor evidently does," he mused, as he sat on the couch his first evening; but from what the guv'nor said, it's a certainty that Mademoiselle Yvonne listened to Patterson's movements through that hole by a sound-magnifier. If she contrived to do that I guess I can, I'll go down now and get some materials from the electrician. I can make one after the pattern of the guv'nor's which ought to do the trick."

Tinker suited the action to the words, and ten minutes later was wheedling a small battery, wire, and other things necessary for his purpose from the gruff electrician. He stole back to the cabin with his materials, and set to work to make a rough, but serviceable, sound reproducer.

Into a small battery-box he fashioned a sounding-board, and then attached his battery. After that he snipped off a couple of lengths of wire which he attached to the battery, letting one end fall free, while the other he coiled and passed through the partition. While the electrician had been searching for a battery Tinker had commandeered an old telephone-receiver, which he connected up to the loose hanging wire. The reproducer had been the most difficult to get, but with a small piece of mica and a hollow steel wire guard he had made a passable substitute.

Tinker scouted about on the deck until he saw Patterson safely ensconced at a game of cards in the smoking-room, and then he slipped down to his cabin again to fix his reproducer. He found the hole left by Yvonne was a trifle small for his steel tube, and had to cautiously enlarge it before he could go ahead. Then thrusting it through he squatted on the couch and pressed the receiver to his ear.

Although the sounds which his hastily constructed instrument carried so plainly to his ears, told Tinker his reproducer was a success, he heard nothing beyond a few grunts and muttered curses until they had docked in New York. Then, while all the ship was a bustle of departing passengers and visitors who had come to meet friends or inspect the newest ocean leviathan, Tinker turned the key in his cabin, and, with the receiver to his ear, listened to his neighbour's movements. The sound of scraping and banging indicated that Patterson was packing. Tinker was just about to roll up the reproducer, and get ready to follow the millionaire, when he heard a knock and Patterson's voice calling "Come in!"

"I thought you were the steward," he continued ungraciously. "What do you want?"

"Are you Mr. Cornelius Patterson?" Tinker heard the new-comer ask.

"Yes. What is it you wish?" replied Patterson testily, "Can't you see I'm busy getting my luggage out?"

"I am representing the 'New York Echo,' Mr. Patterson. We got the wireless news about the theft of the jewel which you were bringing over with you, and I thought you might be willing to give me the story with your own lips."

"Oh, you did, did you?" snapped the millionaire. "The wireless contained all I know myself, so clear out!"

"But, sir," persisted the reporter, "have you any suspicions? Such a jewel as that would tempt the cleverest thief."

"Listen to me, young man," snapped Patterson. "You read the wireless message, did you?"

"Of course."

"Well, did you read that during the evening I showed the jewel to the captain and the purser."

"Yes, sir."

"And did you read that next morning, when I opened my trunk to get it, I found it gone?"

"Yes, sir."

"You also read, I presume, that a young lady occupying the cabin next to mine disappeared the same night."

"The impression is that in some way she fell overboard!"

"Oh, she fell overboard, did she?" mimicked the millionaire. "Well, I think differently. I think she is still concealed aboard this ship, and I'm going to have every person examined by the police as they leave, or know the reason why. If that fails, I'm going back to Europe on the return trip of the Mastodonic. Further, the jewel was insured against theft in England for half a million —its value —so the syndicate of which I am the head will lose nothing. Now you know all I propose telling you or anyone else, so clear out!"

And the reporter cleared. The fact that the jewel was insured was news to him, and Tinker, while the reporter tore off to his paper, ruminated on the fact.

"The guv'nor must have imagined some such thing!" he muttered, as he rolled up his reproducer and stuffed it in Yvonne's bag which she had left behind. "I begin to see now why it was important to follow Cornelius Patterson. It was hard to give up that race to Paris, but the guv'nor knew best, as usual. I wish I had old Pedro here to help me keep track of Patterson, but I haven't, and as I hear him going out I'd better hook it after him."

He waited until he heard Patterson's footsteps echoing down the corridor; then, opening his door, he hurried after.

The millionaire paused to speak to Captain Brown, who was being harassed on all sides, and while Patterson waited his chance Tinker sidled near in order to hear the conversation.

"Ah, Mr. Patterson!" said Captain Brown, turning to him.

"I am very sorry, we haven't got any trace yet of your property, but the ship's detectives are co-operating with the dock police, and if any passenger tries to get through the Customs with it they will be nabbed, sure."

"I'm glad to hear that," replied Patterson. "The thing is insured, but I and the syndicate I represent would prefer the jewel; and, besides, I don't know just what attitude Turkey may adopt, and if we can't produce it, I'm blest if I can see how they can be forced to repay the money!"

"Ah!" remarked the captain, thoughtfully, stroking his chin. "I hadn't thought of that. If it's not recovered the insurance company then stand to be the losers."

"Naturally," snapped Patterson. "But what I wished to speak to you about, captain, is a return passage in case the jewel is not discovered here. I still persist in my theory that my missing neighbour has it, and in a ship of this size there must be some spot where she could lie concealed, particularly if there are any accomplices to cover it up."

54

"The ship's detectives have searched thoroughly," answered the captain coldly. "But if you wish to return to Europe you can occupy the same cabin you had."

"Very well. I'm not sure yet that I will go back. When do you sail?"

"The day after to-morrow."

"All right. I'll go along now, and see how the dock-police are making out."

Tinker flashed a look of understanding at the captain as he carelessly followed the millionaire down the gangway. The captain stood looking after them with thoughtful eyes.

"I don't know just what Blake suspects," he muttered; "but I'm beginning to think the leaving of his assistant wasn't so pointless as it seemed to be. I am inclined to agree with the detective that you will occupy a cabin on the return trip of the Mastodonic after all, Mr. Patterson. But I'd give something to know where Miss Ford has gone. What I'll say to the directors I don't know. Forty years at sea, and to have this happen on the maiden trip of the Mastodonic!"

Blake's prophesy proved correct. Patterson was a passenger for England two days later, and Tinker, tired with the two days' continuous shadowing, once more occupied Yvonne's old cabin.

In New York, he had sent a cable to Blake advising him of Patterson's movements and intentions, and later, on leaving, had cabled again. Blake's answer was transmitted by wireless, and read simply.

"Good! Don't lose sight!"

"Not much chance now that we are such close neighbours again," grinned Tinker, as he tore Blake's message into tiny shreds, and let the wind carry them away.

The Mastodonic was going for the record which had been spoiled on her outward trip, and a trifle over two days out from New York, saw half the distance left behind. It was on the third night that Captain Brown sent for Tinker to come to the chart-room. On the lad's entry, he pointed to several slips of paper lying on the chart-table, and said:

"I don't know what your master suspects, or what his plans are, but he seemed keen on having a look at Patterson's messages when he was on board, and after some thought I have decided to let you copy these. One of them was sent by Patterson just before leaving, and the other three have come one each day since we left. They are all the same, but Mr. Blake may see something in them which I can't."

"Oh, thank you, Captain Brown!" answered Tinker, flushing with pleasure. "It will please the guv'nor immensely that I have been able to get copies of them."

"All right, my lad —go ahead. I wouldn't do this, only I feel sure you will be discreet."

"Indeed I will!" cried Tinker, as he bent over the table, the one which Patterson had sent was as follows:

"Sailing to-day. Fear complications. Advise if groundless arrives."

Tinker copied it out, mentally noting the fact that the word 'groundless' had been in the other message which Blake had seen. Then he picked up the others, which were each sent a day apart.

"No groundless. Will advise daily." They were all the same, and he merely made one copy.

"Seems a funny sort of daily message to get, sir, doesn't it?" he remarked to the captain.

"Yes, my lad; and it was that fact which impelled me to show them to you. This theft and the disappearance of a passenger worries me greatly, and it will be a tremendous relief if Mr. Blake can clear it up."

"If he can't, no one can!" said Tinker loyally.

Once after that the captain told him a similar daily message had come for Patterson, and then once more all was bustle and hurry to land. They had made Liverpool early in the morning, after smashing every transatlantic record.

Tinker dumped his rough sound-producer into the Mersey, and, donning a bulky American suit, which he had thought wise to purchase in New York, he followed Cornelius Patterson ashore, looking for all the world like an American tourist. He had been in New York often enough to pick up the American accent and expressions, and to test his disguise, he deliberately walked over and stood in front of the millionaire. Patterson never dreamed the lad was the same who had occasionally passed him on deck and in the passages, and, turning to hide a grin, Tinker followed his quarry to the train.

Patterson bought a ticket for London.

So did Tinker.

Patterson went into the telegraph office.

So did Tinker.

Patterson sent a telegram.

So did Tinker.

Tinker looked over Patterson's shoulder, but Patterson didn't look over Tinker's. Consequently Tinker knew what Patterson's contained. It had read:

"Brown, Horton, Surrey. Landed. Will leave London by evening train."

Tinker's was to Blake, and simply advised his arrival, and a code word had been added, which told Blake he was still on the chase, and would keep him posted. But Blake was not to receive the telegram, as will be seen in the next chapter. Consequently Tinker was left to follow up the chase alone.

The Eighth Chapter. The Trail of the Pigeon—Blake Takes Afternoon Tea.

WE left Blake on the night after the great Hendon-Paris race, planning his next move to locate Mademoiselle Yvonne, and recover from her the Sun's Eye.

His first move was to send Carter to Portsmouth to meet the Thor, which was returning with the official record of the ocean test. Then Blake had another conversation with the president of the insurance company which had ensured the Sun's Eye against theft.

The balance of that afternoon he spent smoking and thinking, bringing his mind to bear on every point which would give him a clue as to Yvonne's whereabouts.

That she was in England, he felt sure. He argued that, had she been on the Continent, and come to England merely to take part in her audacious race to Paris, that she would have been satisfied with simply racing him from Hendon to Paris, and then would have dropped out. But, instead, she had returned to Hendon with him, which seemed to point to the fact that she was lying low somewhere in this country.

"I'll send out an inquiry to every source I have," muttered Blake. "It is just possible that some of my agents have heard something about this peculiar aeroplane, although the Press has contained nothing. To-morrow I'll have a scout around in the Grey Panther, and see if I can find out anything myself. Then, if the pigeon is well enough to fly, I'll take it down in the machine to Horton in Surrey, and start it for home. The Grey Panther ought to be able to follow it and see where it goes."

With this reflection Blake went to bed. Early the next morning he sent out a sheaf of telegrams to his agents, and was preparing to leave for Hendon, when Mrs. Bardell entered with a letter.

"This just came," she announced, passing it over.

Blake merely nodded and glanced at it. It was printed, not written, and bore neither stamp or postmark. Ripping it open, he read the words on the single enclosed sheet, and a grim smile played around his lips as he did so. The audacity of the thing struck him forcibly, and once again he read slowly:

"Mademoiselle Yvonne's compliments, and she would be delighted if her competitor in the Hendon-Paris race would take tea with her next Thursday afternoon at three. Mademoiselle Yvonne also thanks Mr. Blake for the interesting race he provided, and looks forward to discussing the merits of his own machine and hers. For obvious reasons she regrets that it is impossible to append her address, or even give Mr. Blake the clue of a postmark, but no doubt he is clever enough to find her and keep the appointment. She would remind him that he has a clear week in which to do so."

That was all, and as he read it, Blake could see in his mind the delightful bronze head of Yvonne and her silvery laugh as she wrote the mocking note. He examined the paper and envelope closely, but it could have been purchased in any stationer's in Great Britain, so conventional was it. A thorough interrogation of Mrs. Bardell failed to reveal anything further. She had simply found it thrust under the door, and wanted to know, with some asperity, "if he expected her to sit behind the front door waiting for people who stuck things underneath, and pounce out at them before they got away."

Blake dismissed her when she reached this stage, and completed his arrangements for going to Hendon. All that afternoon, until late in the evening, Blake was in the Grey Panther. He had mapped out a regular campaign of flying, allowing a certain area for each day, and that night he reflected grimly, as he wheeled the aeroplane into the hangar after a fruitless journey, that if he was unsuccessful, the Grey Panther would at least get test enough to suit any Government.

Had the search been on the ground, Pedro would have been invaluable; but even his keen scent could not pick up the trail of an invisible aeroplane. Instead, he had to be left at Baker Street, pacing the floor restlessly, probably worrying his great head over the unaccountable absence of Tinker and Blake without him.

The next day was the same. Blake got away early in the morning, and flew in a northerly direction, but beyond passing Whitcomb, who was trying out his biplane, he saw not another soul. From the thousand foot level he worked up by stages until he was nearly ten thousand feet high. He had lost sight of the earth below; no birds were about—he seemed the only living being in a vast, empty expanse, and for all visible purposes the earth might have been nonexistent.

Only the drumming of the faithful engine and the whir of the propellers invaded the emptiness, but it was an ideal place for threshing out a problem which he was facing. Over and over the points he went, while the slim Grey Panther soared upwards and onwards, but although his deductions told him Yvonne had the jewel, and Patterson was playing a double game, they did not tell him where Yvonne was, and for a moment he almost regretted that he hadn't followed her instead of landing at Hendon.

Only his desire to give the Grey Panther a fair test had prevented him, but the mockery of Yvonne's note had spurred him to action.

"I'll work day and night," he muttered savagely. "If it's within my power to keep that invitation, mademoiselle, rest assured I shall do so, and I might take more than tea from your charming, audacious hands. If I can find you, I'll get that jewel before I leave."

That night Blake received Tinker's cable, saying that the Mastodonic was sailing for England, and that he was aboard with Patterson. It was then he cabled Tinker and put off going down to Surrey with the pigeon until Tinker should arrive.

His persistent non-success in locating Yvonne irritated him. Not one of the agents had heard of the silver-blue waterplane, nor had their far-reaching inquiries disclosed anybody who had.

"It's a lone hand," muttered Blake savagely, "and I suppose she is spending her time chuckling at my failure. She'll send me a nice note if I fail."

The days passed, however, and still Blake got no clue. Wednesday night saw him savage and irritable. He had covered every direction from Hendon except one—Surrey. This he had left, intending to combine the pigeon test with it, and make one flight serve.

He realised that up to the present Yvonne had cleverly hidden herself, and with an irritable remark, he made his plans to leave for Surrey in the morning. He knew the morning would see the arrival of the Mastodonic, and he also smiled grimly at the fact that it was Thursday, and Yvonne seemed very likely to triumph over him. But there was nothing else to be done, and he was up at daybreak, prepared for a hard day.

"Tinker will probably follow his man straight on, and if Patterson goes on to Surrey, the chances are Tinker will keep right on there. He may, however, get a chance to come here, and in case he should, I'll leave a note for him telling him it is likely I will be in Surrey as well."

He did so, and patting the disappointed Pedro's head, betook himself in the motor to Hendon with the homing-pigeon in his bag. The bird was now thoroughly strong again, and Blake had given it a fly around the room in order to see if it was strong enough for the test. He spent some time with the mechanic in going over the Grey Panther, and stuffing some sandwiches in the grub-locker, he wheeled the machine out, and once more shot away on his quest.

It was barely noon when Blake, from his chart, saw he was over the Horton Barracks. The fact that Patterson had received a message from Horton made it evident that the accomplice must live in the neighbourhood; but he shrewdly guessed the name Brown to be assumed. Moreover, the many pigeon-cotes which he knew were in the district would baffle a ground search, and he had hit on the plan of making the pigeon show the way as a test which would be irrefutable proof.

He wheeled, and flew beyond the village, and then, dropping to the five hundred foot level, he reached in the grub-locker, and drew out the pigeon. For a moment it struggled in his hand, but the time it had been with Blake told it he meant no harm, and it rested quietly until he let it get its bearings. Then, with a wide fling, Blake tossed it out into the air, watching keenly as he did so to see what direction it took.

The pigeon spread out its wings, hovering and circling for a few moments, and then, dropping a little, it headed due east at a rapid pace. Blake swung the aeroplane around, banking dangerously as he did so, but if he lost sight of the pigeon, his test would be useless. Swiftly the Grey Panther raced full speed after the dwindling bird. It was soon evident to Blake that he could keep it in sight, unless it dropped into a belt of woods which he could see in the distance. The pigeon was making straight for them, and Blake rose a trifle in order to look down upon it from a more perpendicular position.

He saw the bird clear the belt, and then a large farm appeared basking in the noonday sun. On one side of its ample barn appeared the entrance to a dovecote, and as Blake watched, he saw the pigeon fly straight as an arrow towards it, and disappear. At that moment a man appeared at the stable door, his back toward the detective. Blake, not desiring to be seen at the moment, and realising if he flew nearer, that the noise of the engine would draw attention to himself, seized the opportunity of landing on a small clearing which he saw in the wood below.

Volplaning down, he had reached the highest tree-tops, when over a slight hill not half a mile away, he saw a giant silver-blue waterplane slowly rise, her bulk outlined against the heavy green of some giant elms beyond. She slowly turned and made off in the opposite direction, but before she had blended with the blue above, Blake smiled grimly, and leaped to the ground.

"I'm not sure," he muttered, "but I rather fancy I will be able to accept your invitation after all, mademoiselle. This has been a very profitable morning, and if Tinker only succeeds in keeping track of his man, I think to-night will show more light on matters than there has previously been. But in case curious eyes should spy the Grey Panther, I'll just wheel it in under cover of the trees."

Blake suited the action to the word. When he had finished, the slim grey shape, with wings folded, was standing in a shady, mossy hollow secure from prying eyes. Then taking off his goggles and flying togs, Sexton Blake made a radical change in his appearance. A cool spring near by supplied the means of washing the grease from his hands. Then from the locker in the aeroplane he took a small bag, and began his work. A pointed black beard and black moustache turned up a la Kaiser Wilhelm, gave him a distinguished foreign appearance. A fashionably-cut frock-coat and silk hat completed the change, and made him look for all the world a foreign diplomat, and nothing else.

The friendly little spring provided a cooling beverage while he munched his sandwiches, and after clearing away the last signs that the mossy hollow was occupied, he strode boldly through the wood to the dusty road.

•   •   •   •   •

Mademoiselle Yvonne watched the departure of her 'plane Silverwings on a message to Captain Vaughan on the Fleur-de-Lys, which was cruising in the North Sea while waiting.

Graves was at the wheel, and neither he nor Yvonne had emerged from the hangar in time to see the slim grey shape which dropped into the belt of woods not a mile away.

After the big machine had disappeared above, Yvonne returned to the shady lawn and stretched out in the long low chair which was her favourite. Lazily she watched a fat, overfed robin struggling with a huge worm in the middle of the lawn, while pleasant dreams chased each other through her head. Up above in the giant elms the birds twittered in drowsy content, and blended with the seductive heat came the pure odour of honeysuckle. The multitude of cushions at her back, and the magazine-piled table at her side, made it evident that Yvonne intended putting in a lazy afternoon. A dreamy smile flickered across her face as she thought of the note she had sent to Sexton Blake a week earlier.

"Oh, he will be angry," she murmured drowsily; "but I couldn't resist it. He always wrecks my plans, but this time I have managed without him suspecting a thing. I must keep up the farce, and order tea for two to be served at three sharp. Then what a regretful note I can send him."

The staid, old butler was passing on the terrace just then, and Yvonne called him and gave the order. Then she went back to her daydreams, indicative of the nature of which was the pulling out of Blake's miniature and gazing long and steadily at it. Even as she gazed at it her eyes grew heavy with the heat of the afternoon, the miniature dropped from her hand, lying against her white, softly-pulsating throat face up, and she slept.

Yvonne's dreams were of the same tenor as her thoughts with the exception that while waking Blake was at a distance, and while she slept, he seemed to be with her walking up and down beneath the shady elms, as she had often imagined. Still she slept on, and ever so slowly the hands of the great clock in the old mansion crept around towards the hour of three.

At precisely one minute to three a tall, well-dressed gentleman, with his silk hat in his hands, turned down from the terrace and walked across the soft, yielding turf of the lawn until his shadow fell across the sleeping girl.

He stood gazing down at her for a moment until his eyes caught sight of the open miniature lying face up against her throat. He withdrew his eyes at once, but not before they had seen whose face it was, and as the fact was borne in on him his eyes softened wonderfully and the stern lips relaxed. Far up the terrace the butler could be seen with a loaded tray, and the man standing before the sleeping girl coughed slightly.

Yvonne opened her eyes suddenly, and started up quickly as she saw the tall man with the black beard and moustache standing before her.

"Who are you?" she gasped. "What brings you here?"

The man smiled.

"I was rather uncertain whether I could accept your kind invitation, mademoiselle, but fortunately I was able to do so, and, as you see by the clock, I am in time."

Yvonne's hand flew up to her neck, and her face and throat were dyed a deep scarlet, for she knew he must have seen the miniature.

"You—you!" she gasped, in a futile endeavour to collect her scattered wits. "I—I— Oh, it is too ridiculous!"

And she laughed in silvery tones to cover her embarrassment.

"You are too uncanny, Mr. Blake."

Blake smiled.

"Now that I am here, may I sit down, mademoiselle?"

"Oh, I beg your pardon!" she cried, trying surreptitiously to tuck the miniature back into her dress "Sweep those books on to the grass. Ah, here comes tea! As you say, you are just in time, Mr. Blake."

She was once more the cool, self-possessed Yvonne; but neither she nor Blake could forget the incident of the miniature.

They carried on a desultory conversation while the solemn old servant placed the tray and departed.

"Do you take one lump or two?" laughed Yvonne, reckless of the consequences of his finding her, and yielding herself entirely to the fulfilment of her dreams.

"Have you forgotten?" replied Blake, smiling, while an odd feeling tugged at his heart as he watched her slim hands hovering amongst the tea-things.

"Oh, yes; of course I do! Two, isn't it? But tell me, please, Mr. Blake, how did you find me?" she added, as she passed the cup over.

"Later, perhaps," replied Blake. "That's a fine machine you've got, mademoiselle."

"Isn't it! I think it is a trifle faster than yours, Mr. Blake."

"I don't know, mademoiselle. You see, the day of the Hendon-Paris race I had a passenger, whereas you were alone."

"True!" she nodded. "I hadn't thought of that. Mine is a splendid machine, though. The trouble with yours is that like all aeroplanes the engine makes such a noise."

"It won't soon. I'm working on an electric adaption which will do away with that."

"Ah, mine is already so equipped," said Yvonne. "But tell me, please, how did you find me?"

"I must refuse for the present," smiled Blake. "To tell you the truth, mademoiselle, I have been anxious to see you for some few days. In fact, I was looking for you when I saw you at Hendon."

"Ah! For what?" inquired Yvonne.

Blake looked her in the eye and smiled.

"I thought I might persuade you to give up the 'Sun's Eye,' which you managed to secure so cleverly from the homing-pigeon which Cornelius Patterson was sending with it to England."

If a bombshell had dropped from the sky amongst the tea-things it would not have caused Yvonne more consternation than Blake's remark. For a moment she was speechless. She had no idea that he was on the track of the "Sun's Eye," and much less did she imagine he had connected her with the missing Miss Ford who had disappeared from, the Mastodonic.

"How do you know I have it?" she asked tersely.

Blake laid his teacup down and lit a cigarette.

"It wasn't hard to imagine," he said coolly. "When a valuable jewel disappears in mid-ocean, and a passenger with it, it is natural to look for a connection between the two. Of course, it is always possible on a floating city like the Mastodonic to dodge about and escape detection, especially if one has accomplices."

Then, beginning at the discovery of the tiny hole through which Yvonne had thrust the needle of her sound reproducer, Blake went over her movements as he had mentally reconstructed them.

"I think I am not far wrong," he wound up, "except that I am not quite clear as to your movements after dropping through the porthole. Were some blue signal-lights on the water yours by any chance?"

Yvonne nodded, too astonished to speak.

"I thought that possible," continued Blake. "Then my theory that you dropped into the sea and were picked up by your aeroplane was correct."

"Yes," said Yvonne, in a low tone, "But how do you know all this when the Mastodonic was on her way to America and you were in England?"

"I didn't happen to be in England, I was quite close to the Mastodonic, on board the super-Dreadnought Thor, whose wireless operator caught the Press message of the occurrence."

"Ah! I see," nodded Yvonne slowly. "I'll remember to attend to the wireless next time. It was careless of me. But what do you propose to do, Mr. Blake?"

"Well, by all rights, I ought to arrest you," smiled Blake; "but since Cornelius Patterson was playing a double game, and your intercepting of the pigeon and leaving the Mastodonic was really the cause of my ferreting the thing out, I'm inclined to stretch a point providing you give up the jewel."

"Ah!" breathed Yvonne. "You know, then, what Patterson's game was?"

Blake nodded.

"Yes! Why were you on his track? Was he one of the men for whom you are risking your freedom to be revenged upon?"

"Yes; he was one of the crowd in Australia who ruined us."

"I see. Well, Tinker is on his trail, and I think my evidence will put Mr. Cornelius Patterson out of the way for a little time. He was endeavouring to get the jewel for himself, and make the insurance company pay for it, in order that the syndicate wouldn't lose. Of course, if you refuse to give it up, I will have to adopt means to get it."

Yvonne's eyes dropped to the ground, and a slow flush spread over her face as she plucked nervously at her dress.

"I'll give it up, Mr. Blake, since Patterson will be prosecuted by the insurance company, but on one condition."

"What is it?" asked Blake.

"That you come and walk with me for half an hour under the elms."

"I will be delighted to do so!" replied Blake quietly, reading her thoughts.

Yvonne's hand trembled slightly as she placed it on Blake's sleeve, but she was happier than she had been for many a long day.

While they paced under the elms Blake told her of the proximity of Patterson's accomplice, and how he expected Patterson to reach Horton that night with Tinker at his heels.

"I never dreamed of such a thing," replied Yvonne, "but if that is the case, let me come with you, please, when you go over. Stay here to dinner, Mr. Blake. The train from London doesn't reach Horton until nine, and we will have plenty of time."

"Thank you; I will!"

"Ah, that will be nice!" said Yvonne simply, her hand tightening on his arm. "And, Mr. Blake, at your place at dinner you will find the Sun's Eye."

And Blake did.

Blake stood gazing down at Yvonne.

"Hands Up!"

Discovery seemed inevitable

The Ninth Chapter. Tinker Loses His Quarry —A Long Chase — Found Again.

AFTER sending off his telegram to Blake, Tinker hastened out after his quarry, who was pacing up and down the platform, waiting for the London train to start.

He appeared thoroughly unconscious of the presence of the lad in American clothes who passed and repassed him, and as Tinker strolled by for at least the twentieth time, he chuckled under his breath.

"Tracked him to New York and back again," he muttered, "and he hasn't twigged yet!"

But Tinker was shouting before his horse passed the judges' stand, speaking metaphorically. If the lad had been satisfied to watch his man from a safe distance, all might have been well; but Patterson was no fool, as his business associates might have proved. The persistency with which he met the lad finally caused him to take unconscious notice of his features. From that his mind jumped to the fact that there was a vague; familiarity about them. To a man who was capable of conceiving the plan of using a homing- pigeon for his purposes, it was not much of a jump to the point where he began to wonder where he had seen the lad before.

Slowly his mind worked back to the Mastodonic, and he remembered him as a fellow-passenger from New York. The memory of the features seemed to go back past that, however, and as he sent his mind over every detail of his movements in New York, he suddenly remembered that a lad had been lounging near him in the cable office when he had cabled to England to his accomplice.

As he passed Tinker the next time, he mentally stripped him of his disguise, and drew a quick, whistling breath as he realised, not only had he seen the lad in New York, but he had also seen him in his own cabin, where the strange officer of the Mastodonic had asked such pertinent questions, regarding his trunk, and the two ventilation holes at the back of it.

"Is it possible," he growled, as again Tinker passed— "is it possible that officer was a ship's detective, and that he can have suspected anything? I'll swear that is the same lad who was there at the time. My heavens, if they have suspected me all along! I'd better play warily. But, surely if they did, they would send an older man on

68

the trail than that boy. By heavens, if I had suspected anything on board, the Mastodonic would have had another missing passenger! I can't take the time now to double about. I can't imagine what has become of the pigeon, unless Brown is playing me double, and I don't think he dare do that. But if he is, I'll settle him quick. I'd give something to know what became of that missing woman who had the next cabin to me.

"I wonder if she by any chance really did have any suspicion of the jewel. She might have seen me send the pigeon off, and put up a bluff that she had disappeared, in order to catch the first steamer from New York back to England, and try to get some trace of it. Anyway, her disappearance was fortunate for me. It enabled me to throw suspicion on to her. But what can be the trouble? It was a long trip for the pigeon, it is true; but it was possible. I can't imagine— Thunder, there is that boy again! I must give him the slip in London."

He wheeled and entered a first-class compartment, and Tinker, all unsuspicious that his quarry was on his guard, entered the same carriage, and sank into a corner.

Patterson took no notice of Tinkers presence on the journey. Had they been alone, it is most probable that it would have gone hard with the lad. A buxom, elderly woman, however, also occupied a seat, and little did she realise that her presence was the means of averting what would undoubtedly have been a struggle till death.

At London both Tinker and his quarry arose, and donned their coats with simulated carelessness, but the lad proved to be sharper than Patterson deemed him, and quite worthy of his master's long training. As they crushed out of the narrow door Tinker spied the corner of a handkerchief sticking out of Patterson's pocket.

Little dreaming it would later be his only clue to his quarry's whereabouts, and only taking it in conformance with "Blake's persistent poundings never to neglect details, no matter how small, Tinker stuffed it in his pocket, and kept on after his man. Up the platform they went until they reached the line of taxis.

Here Patterson entered one, and Tinker tumbled into another, not knowing Patterson was keeping a wary eye on him through the glass at the back of the taxi. When quite convinced that his suspicions were correct, and that Tinker was really following him, Patterson picked up the speaking-tube and spoke to the driver.

"A sovereign over your fare if you lose that yellow taxi behind," he snapped.

And the sudden increase of speed, together with the driver's nod, told him the man would do his best. If he failed— well, there were other ways; and Patterson leaned back, and lit a cigar, peering back through the window from time to time, to see how the chase was going.

Tinker's driver merely had orders to keep the head taxi in sight, and, not thinking the other driver knew he was being followed, had let some distance stretch between them, trusting to his eyes to follow the vivid red of the front machine.

That carelessness was his undoing. Tinker, also watching his quarry through the front window, saw him suddenly quicken his speed, and the lad at once grew suspicious that Patterson was aware he was being shadowed. He jerked down the tube, and yelled through it to the driver.

The intervening space, however, was fatal, and as a big policeman held up his hand for the traffic to stop, Tinker saw the other taxi shoot on, the last vehicle through.

With an exclamation, he ordered the driver to go on to Baker Street, as soon as the traffic was released.

"Anyway," he muttered, as they drove along Oxford Street, "I've got his handkerchief, and if he takes the evening train for Horton, I can pick his trail up with Pedro, and follow him, even if he is disguised. I wonder how the dickens he twigged I was following? I am certain he didn't know it on board. It's a good thing I did as the guv'nor has always maintained a detective should. If I hadn't pinched his handkerchief, I couldn't even put Pedro on the trail now."

The cab pulled up at Baker Street, and Tinker hurried in, after paying the man, hoping to find Blake at home. He was doomed to disappointment, however, and found instead Blake's note, written early that morning, saying he was going to Surrey to try the pigeon test. Underneath was Tinker's wire from Liverpool, still unopened.

"Well, if Patterson does as he said he would in the telegram I read over his shoulder, he will go on to Surrey, and the guv'nor's presence there will be fortunate, providing I can locate him, or he hasn't left on his return. I'll get these rags off, and get into a disguise that will fool Mr. Cornelius Patterson, and then I'll make for the train with Pedro."

Pedro had exhibited unusual signs of joy when Tinker dashed in, for it had been a lonely week for the big hound. Ever since the lad had sat down at the desk, he had been sitting with his head on Tinker's knee, begging, with as much intelligence as his great eyes would convey, that he be allowed to go along. As Tinker laid Blake's note on the desk, he looked down and read the look.

"It's all right, old chap," he said, pulling Pedro's ears. "You can come with me to-night, and I guess you'll have your work cut out for you."

Pedro's tail pounded on the floor, and he followed Tinker to his room, where the lad got into the disguise of a young farm lad.

"This will create no suspicion," he mused, as he tugged at the heavy boots. "I might be some farm-hand up to London for the day, and as I'll travel third, and trust to picking up his trail after the train reaches Horton, Patterson won't even lay eyes on me."

Five minutes later, with Pedro on the leash, he was at Victoria, standing in the shelter of a big baggage truck, watching every man who approached the Horton train. His watch was fruitless, however; and when it wanted only two minutes to the time for the train to leave, he began to fear his man had again given him the slip.

Drawing out Patterson's handkerchief, which he had carefully wrapped in paper, he held it to Pedro's muzzle, and then sent the bloodhound up and down the full length of the train. A minute passed, and still Pedro got no trail. Another half-minute passed, and Tinker risked letting Pedro poke his nose in the open doors of the carriages, but the dog only worried hopelessly. As the guards closed the doors and shouted, "Stand clear, please!" Tinker drew back in dismay, and watched the train pull out.

"Well, by thunder, that beats me!" he muttered. "That is the train he said in his telegram he would take, and there isn't another one stopping at Horton to-night. But I'm certain he couldn't have been aboard. Pedro would have picked up his trail somewhere. Now where can he be? Great guns! Why didn't that occur to me? If he got suspicious of the taxi following, he might drop all idea of going by train, and motor down instead. I'll bet dollars to dough-nuts that is what he has done! All right, Mr. Patterson; I may be going on a wild-goose chase, but the guv'nor's got the aeroplane, and the car is in the garage. I'll take it, and go to Horton, and try to pick up the trail there."

It happened that Tinker had hit on exactly that which Patterson had done. On thinking things over, he remembered seeing Tinker in the telegraph-office at Liverpool, and, in case the lad had seen any part of his message, he decided it would be safer to motor down. Had it been possible to give up the trip altogether, he would have done so, but he was suspicious of his accomplice; and could not rest until he had solved the mystery of the homing pigeon's non-appearance. Consequently, while Tinker was pursuing his fruitless search at the railway-station, Patterson was speeding along in a motor bound for Horton.

Tinker lost no time in getting a taxi, and dashing back to the garage. The big, well-known grey car was always kept ready for any emergency, so he was not compelled to waste time in getting it ready for the trip.

Turning on the lights, and pressing the button which released the compressed air and started the powerful engine, he threw in the clutch and backed out. Pedro lay at his feet while they bounded along through the outer fringe of London, and from time to time he rose and poked his nose over the edge of the car, as though he realised they were endeavouring to pick up the scent which had baffled him at the train.

Tinker did not stop to make any inquiries, however, until he had covered a good twenty miles, and then he pulled up at a small inn, which was the main centre of a village through which he was passing. A car had passed through not an hour before, and—yes, he was on the right road for Horton, in Surrey. With hurried thanks, Tinker leaped into the car, and again they dashed on. Only once more did he stop to hear almost a repetition of his first information.

"I'll bet it's Patterson, old chap!" he said to Pedro, as he leaned over the wheel, and gradually increased his speed. "We'll keep after the car ahead, anyway, until we make sure."

Pedro pounded his tail in reply, as though to signify his thorough accord with his master's intentions.

Horton, named after a prominent family whose estate had once embraced the whole district, was almost barren of lights as Tinker swept up its main and only street, for the inhabitants were early risers, and consequently retired while the evening was yet young.

A constable, however, informed Tinker that a car had barely passed up the street ahead, to the garage at the inn, and Tinker, disregarding the officers suspicious look, drove cautiously on. Up the street a few hundred yards he saw the light which shone out from the inn, and a dark blotch on the side towards him indicated the presence of the yard entrance.

He risked arousing the suspicions of his quarry, and turned in. There, sure enough, was the car standing to one side, her lights out. Tinker drove in behind it, and stopped his engine. Then, turning out the lamps, and throwing on the emergency brake, he slipped out, and stole along to the car ahead. Quickly he passed his hand along the bonnet, and smiled in satisfaction.

"Engine still warm," he muttered. "This is the car all right. And now for the man who drove it."

Once more he put the handkerchief against Pedro's muzzle, and then, with the dog on the leash, gave him his head. Pedro went direct to the front seat of the motor Tinker had followed. Then he climbed up and across, leaping to the ground at the other side, with Tinker after him, muttering triumphantly:

"By thunder, I was right! Pedro has got the trail this time."

From there Pedro went quickly along, head down, until he came to a pause at the inn door. As he started to enter, Tinker pulled him back, and just then the hound caught the scent again, a little distance away.

"Ah! He's been in, and out again." muttered Tinker, as Pedro turned and trotted confidently down the dark road.

Once more they passed the policeman, who looked curiously at them, and cast his lantern in their direction, but Tinker ducked and hurried on.

Pedro travelled without fault along, through the village and past its outskirts, until they entered a belt of woods. At that moment, just emerging from the woods, and silhouetted against the sky, Tinker saw a man whose walk told him it was his quarry.

"Crikey! I do wish I could find the guv'nor!" he muttered. "But I suppose he went back to London before dark. All I can do is to follow my man, and wire the guv'nor in the morning."

He had just reached the further edge of the wood, and some distance ahead could see his man turning and entering a gate at the side of the road. The black bulk of the house and barns told Tinker it was a big farm, and, dragging Pedro off the scent, he also turned aside, intending to circle around and reach the buildings from the rear.

Pedro showed an indisposition to leave the scent, but Tinker persisted, and they turned into the woods.

At that moment a soft, peculiar whistle sounded ahead in the shadow of the trees, and before Tinker could prevent it, Pedro had jerked the leash from his hand and dashed ahead.

"Crikey! That was the guv'nor's whistle, or I'll eat my hat!" muttered the lad. "Pedro wouldn't have done that unless it were."

Softly Tinker whistled—a peculiar bar which only he and Blake used—and when the answer came back he knew was right.

"What luck!" he muttered in delight, as he cautiously wound his way through the bushes. "is that you, guv'nor?" he whispered, as loud as he dared.

He almost jumped when Blake's voice came from near at hand, and then Pedro's head touched his knee.

"Yes, Tinker. Drop down in here, my lad."

"How did you know Pedro and I were near?" asked Tinker, as he sank to his knees.

"I saw your silhouettes against the sky," replied Blake. "Was that Patterson you were following?"

"Yes, guv'nor. He gave me the slip in London, but I picked him up again all right."

"Good boy! I looked for you and your man this evening."

"But, I say, guv'nor," said Tinker, leaning forward, "Is that a shadow, or someone behind you?"

Blake laughed.

"No, it is someone, my lad. Perhaps she will tell you herself."

"Can you recognise my voice?" came a soft, laughing voice over Blake's shoulder.

"Merciful Caesar! I beg your pardon, but is it Mademoiselle Yvonne?"

"Right first time," she said softly. "Pedro recognised me more quickly than you."

"Well, you were the last person I expected to see!" answered Tinker. "Is she—is she—" he began, turning to Blake, and hesitating on the words.

"You mean, is she friend or foe?" asked Blake, in an amused tone. "She is a friend to-night, my lad. But no more talk at present. Our man has entered the house, and after a few minutes we must go forward. It is lucky I saw you, Tinker. I want to get both of them. But there may be more.

"Now this is my plan. I will go ahead, and you, Mademoiselle Yvonne and Pedro follow quietly. Keep out of sight, but near, and on no account rush up unless you hear me either call or fire. Do you understand?"

"Yes, guv'nor. But suppose they get you from behind?"

"If you hear nothing by what you consider ten minutes, then go ahead, but not unless. Now I will be going on. Wait until I get across the first fence, then follow, and stick to the shadow."

The Tenth Chapter. Blake Moves—Pedro's Disaster—The Great Fight in Mid-Air—The End.

WITH a final word of caution to his companions, Blake slipped out of the bushes and stole over the fence, the barely perceptible noise of his movements blending with the soft rustle of the leaves and branches as they fell back into place.

There were two small paddocks and three fences to be crossed before he could gain the shadow of the buildings. But Blake was a past master in the art of scouting. Dropping to the ground, and taking advantage of every mound and shadow, he crept along until he reached the second fence. A dilapidated farm waggon, which had been left standing in the paddock against the fence formed a convenient bulk for covering his movements in climbing over. Without its background, his silhouette could have been seen by any suspicious eye, but so carefully did he work that not even Tinker and Yvonne were aware of his exact position.

It was when the last and riskiest fence had been crossed that Blake needed to use his greatest caution, and half-way across to the barn he thought discovery was certain. The kitchen door flew open, sending a flare of light into the yard, and as Blake sank close to the ground he perceived two dark figures outlined against the light. Then the door slammed, and the crunch of heavy footsteps sounded coming across the yard in the direction of the barn.

Blake, looking like a log against the ground, slipped his hand into his pocket and gripped his revolver. Discovery seemed inevitable, but he breathed easier as the footsteps passed on without pause and entered the black opening of the barn door. For the moment he had forgotten that their eyes, coming from the lighted kitchen into the dark yard, had not got sufficiently accustomed to the change to notice him.

He wriggled forward over the turf until he reached the side of the barn, but stopped again as the sound of voices came to him.

"Do you take me for a fool?" demanded one voice angrily, and Blake recognised it as Patterson's.

"Well, you can believe it or not, just as you wish!" snapped the other—evidently the farmer.

"But it is all rot, and you know it!" blazed Patterson. "Nearly two weeks ago I sent the pigeon on the wing with the jewel strapped to it.

76

I get a wireless from you saying it hasn't arrived. I get to New York, and received further cables saying it still hasn't arrived. I leave at once for England again, and each day you advise me by wireless that it hasn't arrived. I land in England this morning, and come down at once. Then what do you say—that the pigeon arrived this afternoon, and without the jewel." He laughed with angry sarcasm. "You'd like me to think the pigeon was taking a holiday until I returned. But come, Lewis, don't try to bluff me! I have offered you a good rake-off. You thought you could play me double, and make me swallow a yarn like that. But I'll overlook it. Pass over the jewel, and you get your rake-off just the same."

"I tell you I'd pass it over quick if I had it!" cried the man called Lewis. "But I'm telling you the truth. The pigeon landed here to-day. I saw it in the dovecote this afternoon when I went up to feed them, and I tell you it had no jewel. I searched every inch of the place. But if you despatched it when you say you did, where has it been all this time? How do I know you haven't had the pigeon with you all the time, and only sent it from Liverpool to-day?"

Blake smiled grimly as he heard the two cheerful rascals quarrelling. He could have explained to the mystified millionaire that the farmer was for once telling the truth, and vice versa, he could have set the farmer's mind at rest regarding the strange length of time it took the pigeon to reach home.

But he decided to lie low for a bit. The more they quarrelled between themselves the easier their eventual capture would be. He knew now without the shadow of a doubt that Patterson was guilty, for he had convicted himself by his own lips.

What the eventual outcome of the quarrel would have been it is hard to say. Patterson was positive the farmer had received the jewel, and had played him double; while the farmer felt himself in the mystifying toils of the millionaire's cunning brain. He felt that Patterson, for some deep purpose of his own, was using him and bluffing him, and in his blind fear he spoke wildly in an effort to see light.

He was beginning an angry tirade against Patterson when Blake heard a soft rustle behind him, and remembered that Tinker and Yvonne were to follow him. He wished devoutly that he had said twenty minutes instead of ten; but there was no help for it now, and he would have to act at once.

He rose softly, and stepped around the corner of the barn. From his left pocket he drew an electric torch, and from his right a revolver. Then, switching on the torch, and levelling the revolver, he strode boldly into the shadowy doorway of the barn. As the white circle of light fell on the angry, arguing men, the farmer stopped in his tirade, and gave an exclamation of fear and amazement. Patterson gaped speechlessly, first at the light, and then at his companion. What mysterious man or men was behind that blinding light neither of them knew, and, as before, they suspected a trap set by the other.

They swung round, and would have volleyed forth recriminations and curses at each other, but stopped as a cold voice came from behind the light.

"Don't move, either of you. You, Mr. Patterson, keep your hands out of your pockets, and you, Mr. Farmer Lewis, don't look so longingly at that hayfork. I hate to see two worthy individuals like you doubting one another; but, really, I think I ought to inform you, Mr. Lewis, that Mr. Patterson has for once told the truth.

"According to schedule he despatched the homing-pigeon from the English Channel with the jewel attached. And I don't mind informing you, Mr. Patterson, that Mr. Lewis also spoke the truth when he said the pigeon had only arrived to-day without the jewel.

"So you see, my friends, you are both truthful men. At present, however, the jewel is reposing in my inside pocket."

Then Blake's voice turned to a steely snap.

"Cornelius Patterson, I arrest you, in the name of the King, for attempting to swindle the Central Insurance Co. out of half a million pounds. And you, Lewis, will have to come along as his accomplice."

Both men stared stupefied at the light which hid the owner of that icy, mysterious voice in its shadow. Patterson was the first to recover his wits, and spoke in a husky whisper:

"Who are you?' he gasped.

"Sexton Blake—at your service!" came the voice. "I had the pleasure of meeting you before, Mr. Patterson, when I made an examination of your trunk, which had holes pierced in it to provide ventilation for cigars."

"Ah!"

The cry came from Patterson, who had gone livid with rage. Risking all in one mad leap, he dashed forward, calling to his companion. His voice and movement brought the farmer out of his trance with a jerk, and he jumped for the hayfork.

Blake didn't wish to fire unless it was absolutely necessary, consequently, when Patterson leaped forward, the detective whistled shrilly for Tinker, and shouted sharply:

"Back, back, Patterson! I'll fire if you don't. There are more with me, and you are only making your case worse. Back, you—"

He broke off and dodged, as Patterson jerked out a revolver and took a flying shot. Blake refrained no longer as he heard the bullet whistle past his ear. Levelling his automatic, he fired, but at that moment something long hurtled through the air and knocked his aim aside, the revolver going off harmlessly into the air as it dropped from his hand.

It was the hayfork which the farmer had thrown in a frenzy, and, with his revolver lying on the floor, Blake stood helpless before the levelled aim of Patterson, who was preparing to fire again.

The pointing of his revolver made it obvious that he intended wasting no time in putting the detective out of business, and, in a last effort to save himself, Blake dashed the torch full in Patterson's face. It was not before Patterson had pulled the trigger, however, and things would have gone very hard with Blake, but for an unexpected occurrence behind him.

Tinker and Yvonne, with Pedro on the leash, had crept across after Blake, and held themselves in readiness to dash forward to his assistance. As arranged they were only to follow him sooner than arranged if they heard a shot, but when Blake whistled, Tinker leaped to his feet and led the way.

As they dashed in through the open door they took in the situation at a glance. The farmer was in the very act of hurling the hayfork at Blake, and Tinker, levelling his revolver, fired at the very moment Blake had done so. Pedro, unfortunately, pulled slightly on the leash at the moment, and Tinker's bullet flew wide.

Before he could turn to his master's assistance, Blake's revolver had dropped from his hand, and Patterson was preparing to fire. It was when his revolver spoke, and Blake, in a last effort to save himself, dashed the torch into his adversary's face that the unexpected happened. Yvonne had drawn her revolver, and an infinitesimal fraction of a second before Patterson fired she fired also. Her bullet struck the gleaming barrel of his revolver, and, glancing along, tore a livid furrow in his hand. His finger barely had time to pull the trigger when the bullet struck him, but the shock against the barrel was sufficient to spoil his aim, and Blake was saved.

Lewis, who had regained his nerve, and realised just how desperate their situation was, turned to Patterson with a cry, and shouted: "Follow me!"

He kicked the fallen torch as he spoke, and broke the current, plunging the stable in darkness, but not before his companion had seen which way he was going.

Blake, in fear that Yvonne or Tinker might fire, called sharply:

"Don't fire yet. Come on!"

But it was easier to say "come on" than to do so. A hurried scraping in the darkness told them that the farmer and Patterson were moving, but in what direction they could not tell. Blake dashed forward blindly with the others at his heels, but Tinker was busy with his pocket and to good purpose.

Drawing out a small torch, he fumbled with the button. A moment later he was sending a wavering patch of light around the barn. No sign of their adversaries was to be seen, but as he threw the light at a rough set of steps in the corner, he saw a pair of heels disappearing through a trapdoor above. Blake and Yvonne saw them at the same moment, and Blake made fresh plans with lightning-like rapidity.

"Give the torch to mademoiselle, Tinker," he called. Then he turned to Yvonne. "Watch the stairway, mademoiselle!" he jerked. "The torch will keep things lighted so they can't attack you in the dark, and you have your revolver. Come, Tinker, they will endeavour to leave from a top window. We must head them off."

Yvonne nodded, and grasped the torch from Tinker's hand as he tore out after Blake. Outside all was still, and against the starlit sky Tinker saw Blake hold up his hand for caution. He pulled up close behind his master.

"Which way do you think they would go, guv'nor?" he whispered.

"I don't know yet," breathed Blake. "There may be a back window opening on to that low shed at the rear. On the other hand, you can see from here the barn joins the back of the house by a passage. Take Pedro, and work quietly around the house, Tinker. If you see them, call or fire. I will work around the back of the barn, and signal in the same way. I think mademoiselle has nerve enough to hold the stairs."

Tinker stole one way with Pedro, and Blake another. Outside and inside dead silence still reigned, and but for the creeping forms of Blake and Tinker, one would never have imagined that there were five human beings playing a tense waiting game of hide and seek about those silent farm buildings. Blake found no sign of the fugitives at the rear.

The low shed was a lean-to of the bigger one, and from the moving and heavy breathing inside. Blake knew it to be a cow-shed. As he thought might be the case, a window in the loft opened on to it, but it showed no signs of having been raised by the fugitives.

He began working slowly around to meet Tinker, when he heard a shout from the lad, and the crashing of bushes ahead. Dashing recklessly around, he gained the road just in time to see two shadowy figures tearing away at top speed, and then disappear into the woods. For a bare second he caught the silhouettes of Tinker and Pedro as they dashed in after, and, with another shout to Yvonne, Blake tore after.

The strategy employed by the farmer and Patterson was suddenly plain to him. They had crept softly through the passage connecting with the house, and while the three watchers were trying to watch every point of house and stables, they had dashed out of the front door of the house which was in Tinker's area.

That the lad and Pedro had lost no time in tearing after them was evident, and as Blake thought of the desperate condition of Patterson's mind and the shot which would have been his end but for Yvonne's markmanship, he redoubled his speed.

As he tumbled over a fence, and headed into the woods, he caught a glimpse of Yvonne coming behind, and then he was in the shadow of the trees trying to follow the chase by the noise of crashing branches ahead.

Into trees and bushes he went crashing blindly, getting many a scratch from their branches, but he knew he was at least holding his own.

Suddenly the noise ahead stopped, and he knew the quarry, with Tinker at their heels, must have hit open ground again.

It was so, for a moment later Blake himself stumbled out into the open to see Tinker and Pedro just vanishing over the brow of a hill.

At that moment a gigantic black screen seemed to be thrust

between Blake and the starry sky. In the act of jumping a fence, he paused and looked up. It was Yvonne's plane returning from the yacht, and it was gracefully volplaning down to earth. Blake could see that it would land just over the hill, and knew they must be on the outskirts of Yvonne's place. Not waiting longer, however, he dashed on, but as he reached the brow of the hill he stopped for a second in dismay at what he saw.

The fugitives also had seen the aeroplane, and with the desperation of drowning men, had seized the opportunity presented. Blake saw the two black forms leap to the side of the machine, and grasp it. A moment later Tinker and Pedro were there, too. Pedro, with a leap, gained the interior, but Tinker fared not so well, and with a growl of rage, Blake raised his revolver and began emptying every chamber at the dark figures. What he had seen was a crushing blow delivered at Tinker just as the lad raised his revolver to fire, and a moment later he saw three figures in the aeroplane, their shapes clear cut against the sky as the great bird-like machine again left the earth.

Tinker had dropped to the ground unconscious from the blow he had received, for the butt-end of a revolver had caught him fair between the eyes; but Pedro was still in the machine.

One of the three figures was holding a revolver to the head of the man who drove the machine, while the struggles of the other proved Pedro was putting up a great struggle.

Again and again Blake saw an arm descend on the dog's head, and then he gave another cry. Pedro was lifted up and thrown out, his body hurtling down a full thirty feet to land with a heavy, sickening thud beside the unconscious Tinker.

At that moment Yvonne came up panting heavily, and Blake, who had emptied his revolver, grasped hers without ceremony, and began firing rapidly at the rising aeroplane. The calibre was too small, however, to do any damage at that range, and he finally desisted to listen to Yvonne's excited words.

"Where is your machine, Mr. Blake? We might overtake them yet. They are forcing my uncle to drive them, but if we can get near enough, I can signal him what to do."

Blake thought rapidly for a moment.

"See how Tinker and Pedro are," he jerked. "If they are injured badly, I won't follow; but in case they are not, I will be getting my machine ready. It is only a short distance in the woods. Meet me where we were in hiding to-night, and if Tinker and Pedro are not too badly hurt, we will follow the other machine."

Yvonne nodded, and dashed ahead, while Blake tore off to the spot where he had left his machine. Not caring to risk a delay by losing his way in the woods, he made for the road first, and then made his way into the little mossy valley where the Grey Panther lay concealed.

It was only a minute's work to pull the slim, light machine out and rebrace the wings. Then he leaped in and laid his hand on the engine, waiting impatiently for Yvonne's reappearance.

Every second was of the utmost value, and he was almost tempted to rise and follow the other machine alone. But he could not bring himself to do so until he knew in what condition Tinker was. His plucky chase had at least served to show the way taken by the fugitives, even if his rash attack, single-handed, had ended so disastrously, for even from the distance separating them, Blake had heard the impact of the blow, and he knew the result must have been severe on the lad, if not perhaps fatal.

At that moment the bushes clashed in the darkness ahead, and he called out:

"This way—more to your right!"

Barely had he spoken, when Yvonne came stumbling into the open space, panting heavily from her run, her dress torn by the bushes, and her hands bleeding from a multitude of scratches.

"They're all right," she gasped, as she scrambled in opposite Blake. "Go ahead! I'll tell you the rest on the way."

Blake nodded, greatly relieved, and lost no time in starting the engine. As the propeller whirred with terrific speed, the Grey Panther leaped ahead over the soft sward, as though propelled by a giant's boot; then, as Blake canted the wings, it rose at a sharp angle, clearing the tree-tops by a dangerous proximity. As soon as she was clear of the woods, Blake sent her ahead on the level, and then, when she had gathered speed, he rose again.

At first they could see no signs of the other aeroplane, but suddenly Yvonne pointed wildly, and shouted.

"There she is! See her outline against those bright stars to the south?"

Blake looked southwards, and saw she was right. At first it looked but a huge night bird wheeling in the sky, but he knew it was only one thing, their quarry. He slightly altered the course, and settled himself in the seat to drive the Grey Panther for all she was worth.

Well it was for Blake that night that his search for Yvonne had necessitated so many long, hard flights. In those every part of engine and aeroplane had received a thorough test. Each bolt had been gone over countless times, each nut had been renewed, each brace had been tried, and the engine tuned to perfection. Consequently he knew what he had to depend on, and knowing that, did not spare it.

As the engine drummed at top speed, and they tore after the other black patch ahead, he nodded across to Yvonne.

"Tell me!" he shouted.

"They were both unconscious," she replied, "but I think not seriously injured. I whistled for one of my men, and told him to get others from the house. They will carry both of them there, and attend to them."

Blake nodded his thanks, and said nothing. He knew he owed Yvonne his life that night, by her prompt action in shooting back in the barn, and that fact made no easier the problem which was troubling him.

True, the present occasion was not a case to put into the hands of Scotland Yard. Had she refused to return him the jewel, he would have been compelled to arrest her on the lawn that afternoon. But she had not refused, and, although technically she had stolen it, still it was from Patterson, who himself intended stealing it and defrauding the insurance company of its value.

Her return of it had enabled him to prevent the swindle without causing her arrest, and now he only desired to get his hands on Patterson's shoulders, and a pair of steel bracelets on that individual's wrists.

But he could not forget that Yvonne was still wanted by the authorities. True, at the time she had tampered with despatches of the British, the Prime Minister had technically pardoned her, providing she left England; but that pardon had never been put in black-and-white, nor had it been endorsed by the Home Secretary.

He had once before warned Scotland Yard of her approximate whereabouts, but the information had been received in an ungracious spirit, and if he warned them again, he imagined he would receive the same curt treatment.

Absorbed in his thoughts, his eyes glued on the black patch

ahead, and his ears listening mechanically for the slightest alteration in the perfect rhythm of the engine, he did not see Yvonne's thoughtful gaze riveted on his face.

Womanlike, her intuition told her she was the subject of his thoughts, and she knew her act in saving his life had placed him in an embarrassing position. But just as his mind was working on the matter, so was hers, and while Blake was still pondering the ethics of the matter, she had already reached her decision.

Far ahead the other machine was growing to look more like what it really was, and less like a bird.

Blake dragged himself out of his thoughts as he saw this, and looked across at Yvonne, whose back was towards it.

"We are gaining!" shouted Blake, through the racket. They are heading to cross the Channel, but if we keep on, we will overtake them."

Yvonne laughed.

"She has more weight than we have," she replied. "But, even so, if I had had a passenger, I think you would have beaten me after all in the Hendon-Paris Race.

Blake smiled and nodded.

It was true. They were steadily overhauling the other machine. The weight of the three heavy men in her was telling, and if all went well with the Grey Panther, it would be only a matter of time before they were abreast. But that moment must be before they reached French soil.

Blake sat tense and silent, watching every move of the machine ahead. Below them lay the shadowy earth with an occasional patch of lights to show where a village nestled. A long string of coloured lights told them they were following the railway.

Then, suddenly, far ahead, Blake saw a mass of lights reflected from the blackness surrounding them, and he knew it was Dover. To right and left he could see the powerful gleam of lighthouses, and moving lights beyond, danced and tossed from steamers in the Channel. A bare dozen lengths now separated the two planes. The extra weight was decidedly a big disadvantage to the leading machine, and Blake didn't doubt for a moment that the threat-driven Graves would have been tossed out long before had Patterson or the farmer had the faintest notion of driving.

On and on they went, ever creeping closer and closer, until the nose of the Grey Panther was level with the tail of the other. Dover swept beneath them at that moment, and almost neck and neck they tore along over the tossing waters of the English Channel.

Then, as she had promised to do, Yvonne signalled to Graves, who could now be seen leaning stiffly over the driving-wheel, with Patterson holding a revolver at his head. Lewis, the farmer, crouched behind them, a revolver resting on the side of the car, and pointing in the direction of the Grey Panther.

Less than a dozen yards now separated them, and Blake could see Patterson urging Graves to do something. Yvonne leaned out, and Graves turned his head slightly, regardless of the revolver so close to his head, and probably realising Patterson would not risk his own life by shooting the only man who could drive the machine, unless things were extremely critical.

Yvonne pointed downwards, and then tapped her revolver. Graves shook his head in despair, but she made an imperative gesture, and then fired. Blake, watching closely, saw that her gestures had dominated her uncle even more than his fear of Patterson, and as the great machine began to volplane toward the water, Blake sent the Grey Panther down also.

Patterson stood irresolutely for a moment, and none but he knew exactly how close to death Graves was in that moment. His eyes caught sight of the water beneath, however, and with a movement of anger he swung and began firing at Blake and Yvonne.

Blake was too much taken up with the machine to reply, but as the farmer also opened fire on them, Yvonne began firing also, Blake pressed the lever which lowered the water-floats, and still neck and neck the two machines took the water together.

Skimming the surface of the water, Blake put the Grey Panther straight for the course being followed by the other then he shut off the engine, and by their own impetus they were carried along until with her engine also stopped, the other machine crashed into them.

Patterson, in his rage, had emptied every chamber in his revolver, and though Lewis had one shot left and viciously pressed the trigger, it hit the side of Blake's goggles, and glanced harmlessly off into the water. Then, while the two machines tossed side by side, Blake unceremoniously grasped Yvonne's revolver, and leaped.

Lewis met him with his empty revolver reversed, and struck with all his strength at the detective's face. Blake took the blow on his arm, and kept on, bringing down the end of the barrel between the farmer's eyes. He then wheeled and raised his arm to strike at Patterson, but he was too late. The other was upon him, and they fell to the bottom in a fierce grapple. Blake's right hand with the revolver in it was still free, but his left arm was numb from the blow he had received.

Unless Graves acted quickly, and came to his assistance, Patterson, with the strength of desperation, would overcome him. A lurch of the machine sent them rolling, and as Blake came on top, he dropped the revolver from his hand and struck with his bare fist. It took Patterson on the point of the chin, and his arms dropped as he lost his senses.

Blake scrambled to his feet, and found Graves sitting in gaping surprise, while Yvonne was keeping the Grey Panther's head to the waves. If Graves had been slow to join in the fray, he showed alacrity enough in assisting Blake to bind the two prisoners. Then he sat back and waited, for he was still in the dark and puzzled to know why Yvonne was apparently working in with her arch enemy.

Blake wasted no time in explanations, however, and Yvonne had her hands full with the machine. Climbing across into the Grey Panther, Blake leaned over to Yvonne.

"Can your uncle take them back to Horton in your machine?" he asked. "If so, I can transfer them to the motor Tinker came down in, and take them to London from there."

Yvonne nodded.

"Of course, Mr. Blake. I'm only sorry I couldn't have given you more assistance, for you know how I feel toward Patterson."

"You have helped me considerably to-night already," smiled Blake, "and when we get to Horton, I'll try and thank you properly for saving my life."

"Please don't," pleaded Yvonne, and Blake turned away, silently reading in her eyes the hopelessness of it all. For a bare moment he had entertained an idea of having a long talk with Yvonne, and endeavouring to get her to give up her course; but in her eyes he read the price he would have to pay in order to induce her to do so, and he felt he couldn't pay it.

Five minutes later as a steamer left her course to investigate the strange-looking objects dancing on the water, Graves rose in the air, followed by Blake, and in dead silence they headed for Horton.

•　　•　　•　　•　　•

Blake hurried into Yvonne's cosy sitting-room, where both Tinker and Pedro had been taken. Tinker had a bad bruise on his forehead, but had recovered, and beyond a terrific headache, was all right. Pedro, however, had received a terrific shaking from his fall, and was still too weak to move. In fact, it may be stated here that Blake and Tinker spent an anxious two days before the faithful fellow was quite himself again.

Yvonne had left Blake alone with Tinker and Pedro, but after satisfying himself about them, he turned to leave and look after his prisoners, Tinker insisting on coming with him. A servant met them on the way, however, and handed Blake a note. Rapidly tearing it open, he read the pencilled words:

"Dear Mr. Blake,—Realising the mental struggle you are having between duty and gratitude, I am forestalling your decision. Even while you read this, I shall be on my way for Paris in my waterplane, carrying with me the memory of our eventful, and, to me, happy days together. When you reach London, I will be out of the jurisdiction of Scotland Yard. My uncle goes with me. I hope your assistant and the dear old dog will be all right soon. Good-bye. I wonder when and how we shall meet again?

YVONNE.

"P. S.—Your machine is a better one than mine.

"P. P. S.—The servant who will give you this has instructions to prepare supper for you before you leave for London.

Y."

Blake folded the pathetic little note up, and put it in his pocket. He smiled with a strange tenderness as he thought of her very feminine postscripts, and then, with a sigh, he turned to Tinker.

"Come, my lad, we will have supper before leaving for London. I will drive the Grey Panther, and you can take the prisoners in the motor."

They turned and followed the servant to the dining room, where a dainty supper had been laid out, and while they ate, Blake detailed the incidents of the chase and capture to Tinker.

"But, I say. guv'nor," remarked the lad tenderly feeling his forehead, "there is one point which has puzzled me for ever so long."

"Yes?" inquired Blake. "What is it?"

"Do you remember when Captain Brown and I lowered you out

of the porthole in Mademoiselle Yvonne's cabin on the Mastodonic?"

"Yes."

"Well, what did you discover out there? I crawled out after you left, but I couldn't see anything."

"I found the faint print of a woman's rubber-soled shoe, my lad," smiled Blake, "and from that fact, I knew the missing woman passenger had left the Mastodonic voluntarily.

"If she had been leaning out, and had fallen, there would have been no footprint. It showed that she had climbed down in order to drop into the water noiselessly. But come Tinker, let us get Pedro, and then start. It is late, and the journey will take some time."

•   •   •   •   •

Cornelius Patterson used all his resources to fight Blake's evidence, and had he not convicted himself by his conversation in the barn with his accomplice, he would undoubtedly have got off. Blake's testimony was too convincing, however, and the jury returned a unanimous verdict of guilty. The judge gave him the minimum—three years—but extended his privilege to Lewis, the farmer, and bound him over to come up for sentence if called upon.

The insurance company presented Sexton Blake with a very handsome cheque in token of his brilliant capture, but the satisfaction he felt over the case was as nothing to Blake compared to his sorrow when he thought of the strange, whimsical girl with the wistful eyes who had been both his friend and his foe in the case, and whose note breathed the heartache of a woman.

THE END.
[33200 WORDS]

Note: This fine serial, which has had such a successful run, will be brought to a conclusion shortly. Look out for title of new serial soon.

Serial follows.../drf

Read This First.

Charlie Gordon, an orphaned lad, who will come into a vast fortune when he is of age, is at school at Bingley. Mr. Skuse, his guardian, employs Mr. Collier, a master at the school, to kill Charlie, when the fortune will revert to himself.

But Mr. Collier gets himself into trouble at the school, and the Head dismisses him. Mr. Skuse and Collier visit their paid roughs on board a lighter, followed by Mr. Banks, a detective.

Banks is discovered, and they resolve to drown him.

That same night, Vernon and Pye determine to break bounds, and go to Sandcombe. Whilst there they stumble into a mystery.

(Now read the thrilling instalment below.)

Mysterious Happenings on Board the Lighter.

Vernon and Pye retained their seats on the wall.

"Now, I wonder what the game is? First of all, what do these two chaps want on the lighter, and who are the men they have gone to see?" said Pye. "Did you hear Collier say that his friends found it safer to keep away from the shore? I expect they must be a precious bad lot!"

"I wonder if they would turn out to be the two men we met that day in the woods?" said Vernon.

The suggestion startled Pye so that he almost lost his balance and fell off the wall.

"I say, do you think they are? And if they are, I wonder what—how—how Collier and Skuse came to know them, and what they are going to see them to-night for? I wonder if it has anything to do with Gordon? I wonder, Vernon, if Gordon himself is on that lighter at the present moment?"

"Gordon on the lighter—a lighter!" cried Vernon. "Good, heavens, I never thought of it! Supposing he has been kidnapped, and that they are keeping him there for some reason—supposing Skuse and Collier know all about it— supposing they have paid these men to do the job for them!'

The two boys were trembling with excitement. They discussed

the matter from every point of view

"Some time ago Charlie Gordon told me that, if anything happened to him, his money, of which old Skuse was guardian for him, would go to young Skuse—our Skuse— Sneaky Skuse! I remember him telling me as though it was only yesterday. Now, I have been thinking. Supposing old Skuse has tried to get Gordon out of the way, so that his precious son can have the money—supposing he was afraid to murder Gordon, so got these two men to kidnap him and take him on that lighter and kept him there?"

"But they couldn't keep him there for ever," said Pye.

"No-o; I suppose not. But Skuse is a wily old bird. Suppose he had some plan, and wanted Gordon out of the way for just a little while, while he collared the money and bunked out of the country, or something of that kind?"

"I don't know," said Pye. "It's just as likely that there's something of that kind, and I shouldn't be surprised— Oh!"

He broke off suddenly. A sudden gleam of light appeared on the lighter, and almost at the same moment the sound of a pistol-shot rang out, and so startled the boys that they almost fell from the wall.

"It was a pistol! Someone has fired! Perhaps it was the policeman! Listen!" muttered Vernon.

The lighter was moored out in the middle of the river, and here the river was at its widest; but in the stillness of the night they could hear the unmistakable sounds of a struggle taking place.

Beside themselves with excitement, the boys gripped the top of the wall and listened intently. Then suddenly the sounds of struggling ceased, and the door of the cabin was shut and the light blotted out.

For a moment both remained silent.

"What do you make of it?" muttered Pye.

"I believe they have found out that they were followed, and have killed the policeman," said Vernon, in a low, horrified voice. "There were four of them, and he was alone; he wouldn't have stood any earthly chance. I wish I knew what to do! Shall we bunk off to the police-station and give the alarm?"

"Perhaps they wouldn't believe us. They are such fatheads," said Pye. "My father says—"

"Oh, shut up! Let's think what is the best thing we can do. I know," Vernon went on, after a pause. "Come on!"

He scrambled down from the wall on the opposite side to that on which they had approached it, and Pye followed him.

"There are some boats here. I thought there were. Go carefully, or you'll find yourself in the river. Look out!"

Fumbling and feeling their way in the darkness, they descended the slippery stone steps; and then Vernon, who led the way, stepped into one of the boats.

"What are you going to do?" asked Pye. And for the life of him he could not help his teeth chattering as he asked the question.

"Do? Why, I am going to row over to the lighter and find out all I can. Perhaps there will be a name on it. If there is, we can row back to the shore and go to the police.

"They might believe us if we could give them all particulars of that sort. There doesn't seem to be anything going on now. Look out! Keep in the middle, fathead, or you'll upset the whole concern! Can you feel any oars about anywhere?"

"No!" groaned Pye.

"Well, I can. Hooray! Here we are!" whispered Vernon. "Get into this boat, keep in the middle, and tread lightly. All right?"

"All right!" gasped Pye.

"Then sit down and shut up; if they hear us, or guess that we are on their track, they'll put a bullet into us, too!" said Vernon.

"Do —do-o you think it is safe?" whispered Pye.

"No, I don't!" retorted Vernon; "but, all the same, we are going!"

He shoved off with his oar as he spoke, and in another moment was pulling steadily and noiselessly out towards the centre of the river.

"Can you see the lighter?" he asked after a few moments.

"No; but I think we have drifted down below it. Yes, I'm sure! Isn't there a current, or something?" chattered Pye.

"Of course there's a current, fool!" said Vernon. "How far below the lighter do you think we are?"

He turned round as he spoke, and glanced over his shoulder; then muttered an exclamation of annoyance, for, not having allowed for the current, the boat had drifted some distance below the lighter.

"We shall have to pull up-stream for a bit now," he muttered.

But it was easier to talk of pulling against the stream than doing it; the boat was a heavy one, and Vernon's arms were not of the strongest.

"Cave!—I mean, look out!" whispered Pye suddenly.

They were still thirty or forty feet below the lighter, when once more the yellow rays of the lamp in the lighter's cabin shot out into the night.

Looking, they could see, against the background of light, the forms of a couple of men carrying something between them. What that something was they both guessed instinctively. It was the body of a man, dead or insensible.

The murmuring of gruff voices reached their ears; then it was suddenly followed by the sound of a heavy splash, and the men, no longer carrying their burden, vanished into the recess of the cabin, and closed the door after, them.

In Which They Take a Passenger on Board and Start on a Strange Voyage.

"They've killed him and thrown him into the water!" moaned Pye; and he cowered down in the boat, and covered his face with his hands.

"I can't stand it!" muttered Vernon. "I can't stand any more of this. We'll get back to the shore."

He turned the boat with its nose to the shore, as he spoke, and just as he got the boat broadside to the stream, something struck heavily against its side

Instinctively Vernon let go his hold on the oar, and, leaning over, grasped at the object that had struck the boat.

It was the body of a man. Dead or alive, it was a man's body, and Vernon held on tightly with all his power.

"Lend a hand!" he cried to Pye. But Pye was beside himself with terror. "What can I do? What can I do?" he moaned. "Oh, I wish we were out of it all, Vernon!"

"So we shall be in a moment, into the river, if you don't lend me a hand at once," said Vernon savagely. "Come over here!"

Pye rose obediently, and staggered towards Vernon.

"Now, then, put all your weight on the other side of the boat to balance her." said Vernon.

Pye did as he was bidden, and Vernon, exerting all his strength, attempted to drag the body into the boat.

But the body was heavy, and Vernon was only a boy; the weight was almost too much for him; but he would not give in. The perspiration started out upon his forehead, and rolled down his face.

"Keep well over!" he growled— "well over!"

"I—I am!" gasped Pye.

Once more Vernon put forward all his strength. He raised the body above the level of the gunwale. With a desperate haul he got it half into the boat; one more haul that nearly capsized the boat, and Vernon and the body rolled together into the bottom of the boat.

Vernon picked himself up again, and sat for a moment gasping for breath after his exertion.

"Oh, dear—oh, dear!" groaned Pye. "What shall we do? There's the other oar gone now, and there's the corpse, and—"

"What did you let the other oar go for? You aren't any good at all!" said Vernon. "Do you mean to say you've let it go?"

"I couldn't help it!" blubbered Pye. "It slipped; the filthy thing slipped out of my hand, and it's gone floating down the river; and — and here we are. Oh, if it would only get a little light! And there's the murdered body, and—"

"Hold your tongue!" said Vernon.

He was down on his knees beside the body, feeling it with his hands. At last he found the position of its face, and bent his own face down until it was close beside the dead man's. It required some little courage on Vernon's part to do this; but he was rewarded for it.

"He's not dead at all! He's breathing all right!" he shouted joyfully. "Here, help me prop up his head!"

"I—I don't know where his head is!" said Pye helplessly.

"Well, that's not to be wondered at, seeing that you have lost your own!" replied Vernon. He was growing more cheerful now that he knew that they had not a corpse for a cargo.

"What ought we to do?" asked Pye.

"We ought to get back to the shore and raise the alarm, and get this chap properly looked after, that's what we ought to do; but since you have lost the other oar, we can't, and all we can do is to wait and see what turns up. I only hope it won't be the boat, though."

"I —I mean, what ought we to do for the —the corpse?"

"Oh, the corpse is all right!" said Vernon. "He's breathing easier now. I expect he'll come round presently."

As Vernon had said, there was nothing for them to do but to sit and wait the turn of events.

Carried by the current, the boat was drifting rapidly down the stream. In a few minutes it had passed under the bridge, and had left the town of Sandcombe behind it.

Vernon took out one of the seats and tried to paddle the boat towards the shore; but, after working hard for some time, he was obliged to give up the task as hopeless. The current was strong, and not to be denied, and it carried the boat on and on, while the minutes passed. The last light of Sandcombe had died away in the distance. The lights of Bingley were gleaming ahead.

"I wonder if we yelled," suggested Pye.

"Wait till we get near the bridge; it's no good yelling here," said Vernon.

So they waited till they got near to Bingley Bridge, and then started yelling at the top of their voices.

But it was no good; the boat shot under the bridge in the darkness. They could see for a moment the lights from the windows of the tavern by the bridge, a few more lights twinkling in the village, and then they dropped the lights of Bingley astern, and drifted onwards past field and meadow till they came to Alfredon Woods.

And now the moon began to rise; the intense darkness was dispelled; they could see the dark masses of Alfredon on the light bank, and on the left the low, flat-lying country of pasturage and meadows.

"How—how far is it to the sea?" asked Pye anxiously.

"Eighty miles, I think," said Vernon. "At any rate we shall be there in the morning."

"D-don't say that!" groaned Pye "What's the next place?"

"Lipscombe; it's only a village —three huts and a windmill; it's about two miles down. After that there's Frenshtown— that's about eight miles from here. In any case, we might as well go on to Frenshtown as not. If we could manage to stop the boat here, we could never carry this chap back to Bingley, and we can get help at Frenshtown."

"If we can only stop!" said Pye. "I wish we hadn't come at all!"

"I don't; if we hadn't come, where would this chap be now?"

"He must be beastly wet; don't you think we could get his clothes off?"

"He'd be no better off then. Leave him alone; rub his hands if you like."

A quarter of an hour later they drifted by the little village of Lipscombe. There was not a light burning in the place, and though they shouted themselves hoarse, there came no answer to their cries.

Then on and once more between banks by which the rushes grew high, between low-lying fields; then suddenly, and of its own accord, the boat drifted straight towards the bank.

Vernon leaped ashore, and Pye followed him, slipping back down the bank in his haste, and sousing into the water above his knees.

"What shall we do? Oh, I am so wet and cold! I say, Vernon, what shall we do?"

"How do I know? I wouldn't care a hang if it wasn't for that poor chap in the boat. He will be frozen to death in those wet things, and he ought to be seen to. It's no good our stopping here. Frenshtown is another three miles good down the river. The best thing we can do is to get back into the boat and trust to luck to land at Frenshtown.

It was the only thing to do, so back they both got, and Vernon shoved the boat off, which, once more caught by the current, resumed its strange voyage.

By now the moon had risen in the sky, and was shining brilliantly down on them. Vernon had removed another of the seats, and, giving Pye one, took the other himself, and the two boys, using the pieces of wood as paddles, hastened the speed of the boat.

"I shouldn't care," Vernon was repeating, "if it wasn't for this chap."

"My feet are awfully cold," said Pye.

"Well, think how cold he must be; he has been right in the river. I only hope he will be all right! Somehow we must land at Frenshtown. We shall!" added Vernon energetically. "If I jump out and swim for it we must land there."

At last the town came in sight. Here the river was much narrower than at Sandcombe, and the current seemed to run less swiftly.

"Come to this side, Pye!" Vernon called out; "and when I give the word, paddle for all you are worth!"

He waited until they had passed under the bridge, then gave the word, and at the signal the two boys paddled with all their strength, both using their paddles on the port side. The boat turned, slowly but perceptibly. She turned and approached the shore.

It was hard work, and the perspiration rolled down their faces; but they succeeded at last. For the second time since their voyage began the nose of the boat touched dry land, fortunately within a few feet of a flight of steps cut into the stone embankment. In a few

96

moments they had worked her alongside the steps, and the two boys sprang out.

"What will we do now?" asked Pye.

"Shout —shout for all you are worth!" said Vernon, and set the example himself.

For some moments their shouts re-echoed along the silent and deserted riverside. Then presently from afar came an answering shout; then another from a different direction, and a few moments later two men came into sight, hurrying towards them.

"Thank goodness!" muttered Vernon, for by this time he was wearied out and exhausted.

A third and a fourth figure came into sight, all hastening towards the spot where the boys stood, and a few moments later the first man arrived breathless on the scene.

"What's the matter? Where did you come from? What's up?" he cried.

"From Sandcombe," Vernon said. He pointed to the boat. "Help him! There's been murder attempted. He —he—" And then his senses swam, and for the minutes that followed all was blackness.

At Frenshton — The Arrest—King's Evidence—Too Late.

When Vernon recovered consciousness it was to find himself rolled up in a blanket before a roaring fire. On the other side of the fireplace was Pye. The other occupants of the room were a couple of policemen and a big, bearded inspector.

"Well, youngsters, how are you feeling now?" asked the latter. "Here, Jenks, fetch the whisky-bottle. We'll give them a drop of grog. It won't hurt them."

There was a kettle boiling on the hob, and in a few minutes the inspector had mixed a couple of glasses for the boys, and then, feeling that his task was not properly completed, mixed one for himself and told the policemen to do the same, and so the five of them sat round the fire drinking hot whisky-and-water.

"Well, where have you come from, eh? And who is the chap you had with you?"

"I don't know. We fished him out of the river," said Vernon. "You see, it was this way. He was chucked off the lighter, and we saw him; and then he bumped the boat, and—"

"Supposing you start right from the beginning? First of all, who are you, and where do you come from?"

"I am the Honourable Aubrey Pye," said Pye, from his blanket.

The inspector looked at him curiously.

"What did you do that for?" he asked.

"Oh, that's right enough!" said Vernon "He's the son of a lord—Lord Donnington, don't you know?"

"Haven't the pleasure of his acquaintance, but I dare say he's respectable," said the inspector, with a twinkle in his eye. "Well, go on. What lord are you?"

"Oh, I'm not a lord yet!" said Vernon. "I dare say I shall be one day if I get properly treated. We belong to Bingley College."

"Then what on earth are you doing here in Frenshton? What made you come here?"

"The current," said Vernon.

"Well, if that don't take the bun!" said the inspector, who was a bit of a humorist.

"No; it took the boat. We hadn't got any oars, and there we were, don't you know?"

"No; it seems to me that it's here you are!" said the inspector. "And a nice mess you seem to have got yourselves into, my lord and gentleman! Now, start from the beginning and tell me the truth. Don't hide anything; because, if you get found out telling lies, you'll be put into a dark cell. We've got one made on purpose for liars!"

"Then what are you doing here?" asked Vernon.

The inspector laughed. He could always appreciate a joke.

"He's a smart 'un, ain't he?" whispered one of the constables.

Then Vernon, told the story of their night's adventure, with occasional interruptions from Pye.

"And so you belong to the school where the young gentleman was lost?" asked the inspector.

"Yes; and we thought we would go out and find out something, if we could," said Pye.

"Oh, did you? Didn't think the police were good enough for the job, eh?"

"Well, they ain't very smart, are they?" asked Pye.

The inspector snorted.

"They've done pretty well up to now; but, of course, if you young gents is going to take the trade up, then it'll be a bad look-out for us. Well, did you find out anything?" he added scornfully.

"We did. We found out several things."

"Indeed!"

"Yes," said Pye.

"And might I make so bold as to ask what valuable information you got hold of?"

"Well, we found out where the two men are who kidnapped or murdered Charlie Gordon," said Vernon.

The inspector and the two policemen looked at each other.

"Oh, did you? And how do you know that they were the two men?"

"Well, we are pretty sure of it."

And then Vernon told of how in the darkness they had recognised the voices of Skuse and Collier, and how they had seen a third man following, how in turn they had followed until Skuse and Collier and the other man had boarded the lighter. They told how they, too, had taken a boat, and had heard pistol-shots, and then had seen the two men on the lighter fling the detective —for so they imagined the other man to be —into the river.

"Well, there might be something in it," the inspector admitted at last — "not that I think it's got anything to do with the disappearance of that friend of yours. I shouldn't be surprised if there was some devilment going on, though. You say you heard shots?"

"Yes, distinctly."

"And then you saw two men chuck this fellow into the river, and you picked him up?"

"Yes. Where is he now? How is he?"

"Well, he's pretty bad. He's in the infirmary, I may say. He's very bad," said the inspector seriously. "He ain't recovered consciousness, and maybe he never will. He seems to have been banged about a bit, and his false beard—"

"False beard!"

"Oh, yes, he had a false beard on! And they've took it off and got him to bed, and the doctors are there; so altogether it's a bad look-out for him."

"I should say he's a goner," said one of the policemen.

"It comes of him being banged about, and then lying all that time in his wet clothes, which has brought on fever. Well, now, the best thing that you can do is to go to sleep. I'll wire off to Bingley, and tell 'em there of your arrival; so it'll be all right for you up at the school."

"I expect it will when we get back," said Pye ruefully.
(Another Long Instalment Next Week.)

**Next week's Sexton Blake v. Plummer yarn will be entitled:
"The Great Safe Mystery,"**

my chums, and will provide some splendid detective literature, showing to great advantage Sexton Blake's wonderful reasoning faculty.

Quite a lot of the action of the story is on Clapham Common—that delightful place where so many South London readers have a habit of spending some happy hours—sailing their model yachts, playing cricket, football, tennis, etc., etc.

But, of course, the yarn has nothing to do with these pleasant pastimes. It deals with one of the most baffling safe mysteries ever known, and Inspector Lurgan, of Scotland Yard, is all at sea, until Sexton Blake comes along and makes a few discoveries; then Inspector Lurgan becomes important, and looks wise.

It is a fine yarn, chums, and I am perfectly sure that you will all thoroughly enjoy it. Remember my warning the other week about ordering beforehand.

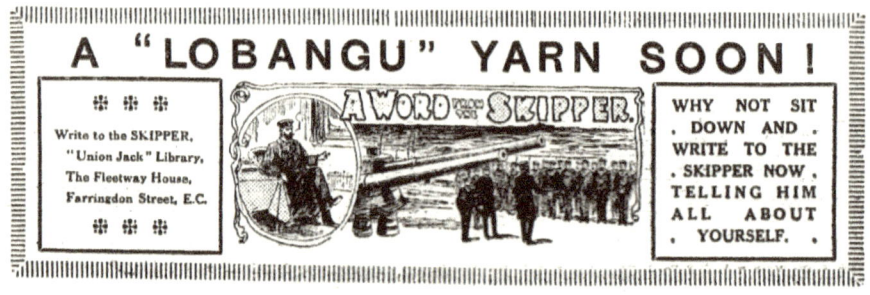

A "LOBANGU" YARN SOON!

✢ ✢ ✢

Write to the SKIPPER,
"Union Jack" Library,
The Fleetway House,
Farringdon Street, E.C.

✢ ✢ ✢

A WORD FROM THE SKIPPER.

WHY NOT SIT
. DOWN AND .
WRITE TO THE
. SKIPPER NOW .
TELLING HIM
ALL ABOUT
. YOURSELF. .

Sir Richard Losely and Lobangu!

For a long time my chums have sent in repeated requests for a yarn introducing those famous UNION JACK characters— Sir Richard Losely and Lobangu, the Zulu chief, so at last I have placed one on the programme.

Everyone is fond of a good, sound adventure yarn, and so the coming story will make a refreshing change, and will give a true and faithful reproduction of life in the wilds of Brazil. And it should be borne in mind that there are great educational qualities in such a story.

That, by the way, is a great feature of *every* "U. J." yarn. It is a recognised fact that the stories contain many valuable hints to the student, and also contain a moral that none of us should flout.

There is no doubt that the wrong-doer *must* come to grief sooner or later, and no matter how clever a rogue one can be, there is a sure punishment awaiting.

But I am wandering from my subject. The title of the "Lobangu " yarn will be

"THE LONG TRAIL,"

so please jot that down and keep your eyes open for the exact date of publication, for those readers who do not order in advance will stands good chance of missing it.

SOMETHING FOR SPORTS LOVERS.

Among that great portion of the community who constitute "U. J." readers, there are doubtless many thousands who are lovers of sport. To them I would recommend the "Sports Library." the finest sporting fiction paper on sale, and that at the price of *one halfpenny!* There have been many achievements in the journalistic world, but surely none greater than that of producing a twenty-page paper positively crammed with sporting fiction of the highest type.

The authors who write for the "Sports Library" know their subjects. If a tale deals with any particular brand of sport, then, depend upon it, that tale is accurate in all details, and reflects, as if in a mirror, the inner workings of that remarkable sphere, the world of sport. To enumerate all the attractions is impossible, in a small space, but the investment of the minute sum of one halfpenny will give you all those attractions. Boxing, football, cricket, swimming, running, all are dealt with in fiction form.

Read of the "Dandy Champion," of the "Three Champions," of "Get-There Gunter"—sportsmen and gentlemen all. To find a better ha'porth is impossible; to go through the week without a copy is, once you have read a number, a penance. Buy now! Your newsagent sells it, as every good newsagent should, and don't forget to ask for it on Wednesday, Thursday or Friday, in the majority of cases, is too late; and never forget the price—one halfpenny!

Another Letter from China.
"Tientsin,
"North, China.

"Dear Skipper,— I hope you will excuse me writing these few lines. Although far from England, I read the *Union Jack,* which I get sent out, and I can say they are very good, especially the Plummer and Carlac yarns.

"In one of your books I see one of my chums asked you about a Plummer and Carlac yarn where the two criminals get together. I think myself it would be all right. And the stories are quite good in your new series, as they get better every time I read them.

"Wishing you the best of luck,

"I remain,

"Yours faithfully.

"W. G. S."

Thanks, W. G. S., for letter. I am afraid I cannot give a Carlac and Plummer story as you and others have asked. Please accept my best wishes.

SEXTON BLAKE IN 3d. BOOK!

At last, my chums, I have arranged to give you a fine long story in the "Boys' Friend" 3d. Complete Library, introducing Sexton Blake, Tinker, and Pedro v. Dr. Huxton Rymer.

The story is entitled "The Great Mining Swindle," and is
NOW ON SALE.

A GREAT SUFFRAGETTE RAID!

The doings of the militant Suffragettes lately have aroused a great deal of attention, both from the public and the police. Therefore, I think a yarn introducing a great raid by Suffragettes, with subsequent serious complications, which involve Count Ivor Carlac and Sexton Blake, would not be out of place.

I have completed arrangements with the author of the famous Carlac yarns, with the result that
"THE CASE OF THE SUFFRAGETTE RAID"
will make its appearance in two week's time.
Look out for it, and order in advance.

THE SKIPPER.

www.ingramcontent.com/pod-product-compliance
Lightning Source LLC
Chambersburg PA
CBHW031852170626
46807CB00004B/1695